Please, please hurry, he prayed

The operator came back on the line. "You may go ahead, sir."

"Walker! It's Liam."

"O'Toole, what do you..."

"I'm in trouble, Walker. Call Barrabas..." O'Toole saw something through the telephone-booth window that froze him momentarily. A man drove into the parking lot on a motorcycle. "Call Barrabas, now! Get him to Susy's house. She needs..." O'Toole broke off as the man dismounted and pulled a handgun from his jacket. He walked toward the Irish warrior.

"Liam, what in hell's name is..."

"Jessup, she's in danger. I'm..."

O'Toole looked up, into the big black eye of the gun. And Seamus Killerbey.

"I'm in..."

The gun blinked.

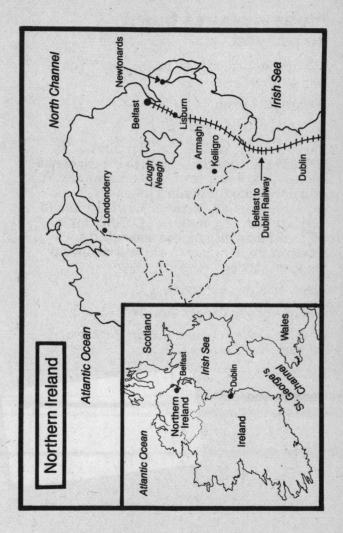

Northern Ireland

SOBs
SOLDIERS OF BARRABAS

NO SANCTUARY

JACK HILD

A GOLD EAGLE BOOK FROM
W⬤RLDWIDE

TORONTO • NEW YORK • LONDON • PARIS
AMSTERDAM • STOCKHOLM • HAMBURG
ATHENS • MILAN • TOKYO • SYDNEY

First edition July 1986

ISBN 0-373-61613-9

Special thanks and acknowledgment to
Robin Hardy for his contributions to this work.

Printed in Canada

1

It was a typical Belfast day, with low angry clouds threatening rain that never came. The funeral cortege, led by the solemn black hearse, wound its way slowly along the narrow cobblestoned street toward the hillside cemetery. People watched from the doorsteps of the grimy brick houses, their faces silent, white and grim. Behind the hearse, a long limousine carried the grief-stricken mother of the fallen hero. Terry McHugh, who now lay cold and stiff in his coffin, had been cut down by a British army bullet two days earlier. It was a fitting death for the Ulster commander of the provisional wing of the Irish Republican Army. Terry McHugh, the latest victim in the struggle that pitted Catholic against Protestant in the six counties of Northern Ireland, joined the ranks of fallen martyrs in the eight-hundred-year-old war between Irish and English.

Even in death Terry McHugh did not find peace. That morning, the British army, impervious to the tears of Terry's distraught mother, had refused to release the body to the family. The authorities knew that bearing the corpse through the impoverished streets of Catholic Belfast would unleash violent sentiments against their rule, sparking riots that might leave scores dead. Finally the family and the authorities agreed upon a route that would bypass the areas of heaviest Catholic population. But now, as the cortege reached the end of its route, the crowds outside the gates of the cemetery had swelled. The people muttered with suppressed anger, scarcely controlling their hatred for the foreign soldiers who had taken the life of one of their own.

At the end of the narrow street, a convoy of Land Rovers braked quickly to a halt and closed the intersection before the hearse could turn onto the road that led up to the cemetery. Men in the blue uniforms of the Royal Ulster Constabulary emerged from the vehicles and sauntered haughtily along the street. Their defiant looks masked the fear fed by the hatred in the faces of the crowd. The paramilitary policemen, who had little but contempt for Ulster's Catholic minority, made a great show of pulling their assault rifles from the Land Rovers and strapping belts of plastic bullets around their waists.

The hearse slowed to a stop in the middle of the intersection, and Terry Underough, one-half of Underough & Slash Morticians, Inc., stuck his head out the driver's window and shouted at the nearest RUC policeman.

"Bit of a problem there, lad? Got someone I want to bury in here and 'e's getting ripe, if you know what I mean. Now if you could just drive that there jeep of yours ahead a mite, we could get 'im planted 'fore there's any problem."

A tall red-faced policeman with sergeant's stripes walked belligerently toward the hearse window.

"Looks like there's trouble brewing, Mr. Underough. Could be a bit of aggro, and we want to avoid that now, don't we?"

The other RUC policemen were listening. Terry Underough knew damned well from their smirks that they had something up their sleeves.

"What in hell are they trying to pull?" Patrick Slash, the other half of the firm, asked from the seat beside Terry.

"Something," he said worriedly. In the side mirror he could see the limousine carrying the deceased's mother slowing to a stop behind the hearse.

"No, sirree, we wouldn't want a bit of aggro now, would we?" the sergeant repeated, smiling broadly and looking back over his shoulder at his fellow policemen to share the jest. They laughed at some secret joke and watched the mortician.

Abruptly the big policeman leaned over and stuck his face in the window of the hearse. "Guess we'll just have to take this corpse off your hands, before it gets to stinking too high and causing trouble."

Terry Underough looked aghast. "What right do you...under what authority..." Before the policeman could answer, Underough knew that no authority was necessary, no rights were recognized and the Royal Ulster Constabulary would bloody well do as they pleased.

The policeman's face grew redder and his voice was ugly now. "As an officer of Her Majesty the Queen I am hereby arresting the remains of Terry McHugh."

"But . . ."

"Under the lawful authority of the Flags and Emblems Act."

The police sergeant waved his arm, and the policemen swiftly ran into position, cordoning off the intersection and surrounding the hearse. Their heavy boots thundered on the pavement, and they raised their rifles, snapping off the safety locks in unison, and held the guns across their chests. Behind the hearse and on the other side of the police line, the limousine doors opened and Terry McHugh's mother and father stepped out, their faces stricken with grief and confusion. Other cars came to a stop, and the rest of the McHugh clan—brothers and sisters, aunts and uncles—emerged and crowded around the bereaved parents.

"What's going on here? What's going on?" Mr. McHugh asked, his voice weak and strained.

The sergeant strode to the edge of the police cordon and glared at the mourners. "We are arresting the remains under the Flags and Emblems Act as liable to provoke a riot. You can all go home, because there won't be a funeral for Terry McHugh today—or any day. And you can take your IRA friends with you."

The policeman pointed to the crowd of sullen men who had crowded out of the cars in the cortege and circled around the beleaguered family. Then he turned back to shout to one of his men, "Get Underough and Slash out of the hearse and let's get it out of here."

Terry Underough locked the door and tried to roll up the window, but it was already too late. The steel barrels of three rifles jammed through the window.

Then a hand came through and pulled up the lock. The door swung open. More hands reached into the front seat and grabbed Underough by the collar of his black overcoat. As he felt himself roughly jerked sideways, he threw himself to the center of the seat. Hands clutched his ankles. Four big policemen dragged him out the door. When Underough grabbed the steering wheel, policemen reached in and smashed a rifle butt across his knuckles. The mortician yelped in pain and let go. He hit the pavement buttocks first. Only the soft cushioned seat of the hearse saved his head from a major bashing.

"Get the keys and get that other man out of there!" the sergeant yelled angrily, pointing toward Slash, who cowered against the other door in the front of the hearse.

On the other side of the police line Mrs. McHugh murmured, "My God, oh, my God, sweet Mary mother of Jesus..."

The dead man's father roared. "Why, you lying, thieving villains..." He balled his fists and ran at the police line, crashing through it and running toward the hearse.

A young constable stepped forward and swung his rifle butt. It connected solidly with the old man's solar plexus. With a breathless oomph of pain, Mr. McHugh collapsed to the ground and writhed in agony. Mrs. McHugh shrieked and burst into tears. Terry McHugh's sisters screamed. The youngest, barely seven years old, began to run hysterically back and forth between the car and her mother. Angry mourners surged forward, and more policemen ran from the Land Rovers to strengthen the police cordon. Back at the hearse, police reached inside the front seat to drag Slash out. The enterprising mortician grabbed the keys from the ignition and pressed himself harder against the locked door.

"Come on now, undertaker," a policeman cooed, reaching toward him. "We're taking the corpse, so just give us up those keys and get out."

"Over my dead body," Slash cried.

"If necessary..." the policeman warned. He grabbed Slash's sleeve just as a rifle butt crashed through the window of the hearse, showering the mortician with glass. Quickly the door was unlocked and opened. Hands reached inside to grab Slash.

Slash looked at the policemen and at the policemen's guns. Then he looked at the keys that he held in his hand. A policeman reached for them. Slash plunged them into his mouth, took a deep breath and welled up what saliva he could. He swallowed.

They caught in his throat. His eyes grew large as he felt himself choking.

"'E swallowed the bleeding keys!"

"Grab 'is throat! Grab 'im by the bloody throat!"

More policemen reached in and yanked him out of the hearse. Slash took a deep breath and, with an immense effort, forced himself to swallow again.

The thick, heavy lump slid down his esophagus.

Slash looked at the police encircling him and threw them a big toothy smile.

At the edge of the melee, the crowd of onlookers stirred, and their mutterings rose into jeers, slow at first, then quickening and growing louder as their anger gave them courage.

"English Out! English Out! English Out!" The voices merged into a single, syncopated chant. Fear crossed the faces of the Royal Ulster Constabulary again, and they looked at one another and then to the sergeant. He seemed worried.

Mrs. McHugh, still murmuring to her Lord, pushed against the police line in an attempt to get to her husband, who lay on the ground, moaning and holding his midsection. The McHugh sisters wept and sobbed and screamed, while their brothers ran forward into the fists and pointed rifles of the policemen.

Suddenly, from the edge of the crowd, a man wearing the stiff white clerical collar and flowing black robes of a Catholic priest pushed his way toward the red-faced sergeant. The priest was a tall man, and although his dark hair was graying at the temples, he walked with a gait that suggested a powerful and muscular body was hidden under his priestly robes. He went quickly toward the McHugh brothers, calling them by name.

"Now Tommy, Timmy, Patrick, Simon..." Quickly he reached out and grabbed each of them by the shoulder, jerking them back. "There'll be nothing to be gained if we all end up in the Maze, will there be, laddies?" he said, referring to the infamous prison where IRA suspects and members were interned for years at a time. The priest strode forward to the edge of the police line. Faced with the crowd's growing hostility, the sergeant was temporarily immobilized by indecision.

"Sergeant Peterson," the priest called. It seemed he knew everyone by name. "I'm Father Darby O'Goole, the parish priest in Kelligro, where the McHughs reside. It's getting a wee bit out of control, wouldn't ye say? Perhaps we can speak a bit and work this out now."

The sergeant walked slowly to his side of the police line and stared at the priest. His voice was gruff. "And what exactly do you suggest?" There was no respect in his voice.

"Well, now, perhaps you can help me out by telling me exactly what the problem is," Father O'Goole suggested, flashing a hopeful smile.

The sergeant looked at the priest as if the thought of discussing anything with him were distasteful. Around him, along the sides of the street, the people grew restless.

"English Out! English Out! English Out!" The chanting had settled into an angry, ominous beat. Soon the petrol bombs would arrive. Then the sharpened sticks. Then the paving stones would be pried from the streets, and shortly after that, all hell would break loose. The sergeant didn't mind much. After all, he and his men had rubber bullets to protect them. Fired into the faces of the advancing mob, they were effective. But he'd just been through this two days earlier, when Terry McHugh had been shot down. And if there was going to be another riot, it meant he wouldn't be home in time for dinner for the second time that week. He decided to negotiate.

"At the top of this hill, just outside the cemetery, there're three thousand people waiting. And more of

them coming all the time. The mood's getting ugly."
He leaned closer to the priest. His face twisted, uglier
than the mood of the crowd he'd described. "You
know yourself, Father—" he said it with a sneer "—
these people get excited easily. They can't be controlled."

Father O'Goole swallowed, forcing down his pride
and feeling it tighten into a ball of hatred against Ireland's Protestant overlords. He raised his chin. "Of
course," he said smoothly, adding with irony, "and
over so little."

"So we're taking this body out of here," the sergeant said with finality.

The priest looked surprised. He raised his eyebrows. "And what exactly had you planned to do with
it?"

Now it was the sergeant's turn to look surprised. He
hadn't thought that far ahead.

"Er...well..." he blustered.

"Let me help you out, Sergeant," Darby O'Goole
said calmly. "We'll take the body." He glanced back
at poor old Mrs. McHugh, who was sobbing hope-
lessly with her daughters. Her sons looked on with
glaring hatred. If eyes could kill, the RUC would be
dog meat.

The priest continued. "We'll take the body back to
Kelligro, to the McHughs' house. There hasn't been a
wake, so we'll have one tonight."

The negotiations continued for the next half-hour,
with Father Darby O'Goole consulting the Mc-
Hughs. Finally an agreement was reached. The
McHughs would take the body to the family home for

the wake. Then, in the wee hours of dawn, the coffin would be returned to Belfast for a secret internment.

When the decision had finally been made, the police moved aside to allow the hearse to turn around. Underough and Slash found the spare set of keys and started up the hearse. Slash wore a pained expression, anticipating without pleasure the retrieval of the first set—a painful and humbling experience, he was sure.

The McHugh family and the other mourners got back into their cars. The drivers backed up and prepared to return along their route through the poor workers' neighborhoods that made up Catholic Belfast. The chants and jeers from the throng of spectators slowly died as the hearse disappeared down the narrow cobblestoned street.

Father O'Goole made his way back to a white car in the cortege. He opened the rear door and slid into the seat beside a thick, husky man with sandy hair and fair skin. They exchanged looks as the driver started the car and maneuvered it into place in the funeral procession.

"An' as sure as my name's Seamus Killerbey, those bastards will pay for what happened here today," the sandy-haired man said.

"You have great responsibilities now," commented the priest. "There are a number of things we have to discuss regarding your new position."

"Right you are," Killerbey answered. "Now that I'm the commander of the provisional wing of the Irish Republican Army, those RUC bastards will pay in blood!"

SOME HOURS LATER, well after darkness had fallen, the wake for Terry McHugh was in full swing. In the dining room of the McHugh family home, the chairs had been cleared away and the open coffin set out on the long table. The outrage of the afternoon had given way to merriment. The fallen martyr lay resplendent in his dark suit, snuggled by the satin cushions of the last bed he would ever lie in.

"Like a sleeping angel," someone in the crowd commented.

"None the worse for wear, are you now, Terry me friend?" a drunken voice shouted. "Let's drink again for Terry McHugh and everlasting war against the English!"

A bottle of good Irish whiskey was raised into the air, and the golden liquid spilled into glasses. The McHughs had long since retired, exhausted by their grief and the events of the afternoon. The voices of Terry McHugh's drinking buddies—who also happened to be his IRA fighting companions—broke into a traditional Irish drinking song.

"I never did see a lovelier corpse," one of them shouted above the song.

"'E's pickled in Irish whiskey," shouted another. "'Twas always 'is favorite an' 'e put it away like none of us ever could!"

The party was getting rowdier.

Seamus Killerbey lurched away from the coffin and slammed the empty bottle of whiskey hard onto a table. He put his glass to his lips, and felt the smooth fiery liquid burn its way down. It cleared his head momentarily. Then his vision went fuzzy. He closed his eyes and shook himself. When he opened them, his vision was normal again. The men and their wives and girlfriends had joined hands, and with their voices raised in song, they began to dance around the coffin. Killerbey watched with a bemused smile.

"Not too much to drink, I hope."

The soft voice came from behind him. It was O'Goole.

"You have responsibilities now. Heavy ones," the priest continued, moving into Killerbey's line of vision.

"Aye." Killerbey nodded heavily. "We'll have our revenge for Terry's murder. We've made plans already. Belfast will ride a train the likes of which they've never seen before."

Father Darby O'Goole nodded. "There is this other matter...the one that was so dear to Terry McHugh and that he never saw completed."

"Aye. The traitor."

"I am concerned about it. The man is being lured back to Ireland and is due anytime. We await word of his arrival. But our agent has given us some interesting information on these friends of his."

"His line of work... You know yourself that as a professional soldier, a mercenary, he's bound to have some tough friends. It makes no difference. He must pay for his crimes against the Irish Republican Army, and pay he will. With his life."

"It makes no difference," Darby O'Goole agreed ominously, "as long as his friends don't come looking for him. This man, Nile Barrabas, and—what is it they are called, the Soldiers of Barrabas?"

"Aye. The SOBs—also known as sons of bitches. Very funny. Typical of these Americans. They act like children."

"Still," O'Goole said warily, "we can take care of the traitor. As long as his friends don't come looking."

The shouts of laughter and song, and the stomping of feet as Terry McHugh's friends danced around the coffin, almost drowned out the ringing of the telephone in the adjacent room. A woman, one of Terry's sisters, came to Killerbey.

"It's for you."

"Excuse me," he said to the priest.

The noise faded as he closed the sitting-room door behind him. He picked up the telephone receiver.

"Seámus."

It was a woman's voice.

"He's here."

"Where?"

"At the hotel. Just where I said he'd be."

"Alone?"

She laughed. "Except for his wife."

"Tomorrow evening," Killerbey told her.

She laughed again, softly. "He will finally pay for his crimes against Ireland."

"Yes. But first we will use him for our own purposes. Then he will be tried before a military tribunal of the Irish Republican Army. The charge is treason."

"And then he will be executed."

Killerbey thought he heard the woman sigh, as if with a touch of regret.

"You know what to do," he told her. "Be ready."

Just as he hung up the phone the door flew open. Voices and laughter burst into the room.

"Seamus Killerbey! Now what be you doing in here?" the man and woman at the door shouted exuberantly. "Hiding from the party, and your old friend Terry McHugh is asking you for a last dance!"

Seamus Killerbey laughed merrily as the woman waltzed into the room and took hold of his arm. Together they danced back into the dining room. Another glass of Irish whiskey was shoved into his hand. Someone had poor old Terry McHugh propped up stiffly in his coffin, and was holding a glass of whiskey to the dead man's lips. The whiskey dribbled down over his cold bluish skin.

"A drink for the dead man," someone else shouted. "Terry wouldn't forgive us if we left him out of his own wake."

Killerbey laughed uproariously.

"Why an' you're sure happy tonight, Seamus," the woman on his arm said curiously.

"We've something to celebrate now!" he crowed to the gathering.

"What's that?!" someone shouted.

Seamus Killerbey grabbed the woman beside him and waltzed around the dining-room table. He let go of her and looked at the corpse, which was stuck halfway out of the coffin. "One last dance for Terry McHugh!" he roared. "To celebrate Terry's final victory!"

"What's that?" the merrymakers shouted. "What is it?"

Seamus Killerbey, quick with whiskey in his veins, grabbed the corpse of his old friend under the cold hard arms and heaved the body from the coffin. The dead Irish martyr stood rigidly at attention, stiff as a board.

Killerbey bellowed. "The traitor has come back to pay for his crimes. Liam O'Toole, the greatest coward Ireland has ever known, has come back to die!"

The din of cheers drowned out the last of Killerbey's words. He laughed on and on as he swung the corpse in circles around the coffin in a macabre dance of death.

2

Twilight fell, filling the Irish air with a touch of purple before thickening into evening. From the terrace of Ashford Castle, Liam O'Toole gazed across the grounds, past the tops of pine trees at the edge of the lawn. Below the stone walls, the lights in the circular fountain came on. In the distance, a milky mist had settled down over the waters of Lough Corrib, obscuring the islands that floated like dark ships in the lake. The growing dusk extinguished the distant Connemara Hills completely.

"Illauna, Crickedia, Illaundarragh, Inchagoill," the tall muscular Irishman recited. The wind blew his thick red hair into his eyes. The blond woman beside him shivered, and he put his arm around her shoulders.

"What?" she asked, looking quizzically at him.

"Those are the names of the islands of Lough Corrib. Beautiful, aren't they? The sound of the Gaelic."

She smiled at him. "Glad to be back here?"

"Never been happier," he told her. "It's because of you."

Liam O'Toole and his new wife, Susy Rourke, had finally begun their long-delayed honeymoon at a luxury hotel in ancient Ashford Castle on the Cong River in Ireland's County Mayo. The first honeymoon, a vacation in Miami, had been interrupted by the call to battle. Liam's commander in chief, Nile Barrabas, had been assigned a secret mission as an observer to the enthronement of a famous black bishop in South Africa, and the Irish-American had been needed for the job. What had begun as a simple assignment to oversee South African security arrangements had turned into a minor war to stop the white racist Inner Circle from their attempt to assassinate the anti-apartheid leader.

Other missions had followed in quick succession. Liam O'Toole had had enough. He had Susy now. He'd stopped drinking, stopped the crazy womanizing and the binges between battles.

He was starting a new life with a new wife, and all he had to go on was love. About the only skills he knew were fighting and demolitions—his area of expertise—and he didn't know what kind of career he could make out of them. But several years and a dozen assignments with the Soldiers of Barrabas had left him a wealthy man. And he had Susy. The future would take care of itself somehow.

In the meantime, he was going to enjoy the honeymoon in his native country and try to make amends for some of the mistakes he'd made in the past. With Susy by his side, he felt for the first time in years that everything was possible.

He watched her as she contemplated the beauty of County Mayo, stretching away on all sides of the ancient castle. The evening breezes blew threads of her long blond hair. Her skin was fair, her lips full and sensuous. Under the bulky knit sweater, she had a well-proportioned, voluptuous body that Liam O'Toole never tired of exploring. It was sex—pure lust—that had brought them together in the first place. He'd found her through an ad in one of those swinger tabloids, and thought he was going for an afternoon of diversion with a bored New Jersey divorcée. The physical chemistry had been electric, but neither of them had known their encounter would blossom into this incredible romance. It had been the farthest thing from Liam O'Toole's mind at the time. In fact, romance hadn't occurred to him since he was a dumb, towheaded seventeen-year-old in Belfast, running bombs for the IRA because he didn't know any better.

Susy shivered again. A chill had settled with the passing of the sun.

"Shall we go down and have something to eat, me love?" Liam asked her.

She smiled and nodded. "I was wondering when you'd ask."

"Lost in my thoughts," he apologized.

"Penny for them."

"They aren't even worth that."

"Tell me."

"I was thinking about what I want to do tomorrow. Remember I told you I needed your help with something?"

"It's about time I knew what it was."

"Over dinner. Come on."

They walked arm in arm back into their luxuriously appointed, oak-paneled suite, then exited into the wide hallway and descended the staircase that led into the baronial central foyer. A few minutes later they sat under the enormous crystal chandeliers in the dining room, scanning the menus while white-coated waiters scooted back and forth, filling their water glasses and lighting the candles at their tables. Liam watched the reflection of the tiny flickering flames in Susy's eyes.

"It's beautiful," she said. "How did you know about this place? Did your family come here when you were young?"

Liam laughed heartily. "In a manner of speaking, love. But not as guests. I come from the wrong class for that. My father worked here as a gameskeeper for a while, and my mother was a chambermaid. When I was a wee bairn, my grandmother took care of me and my brothers and sisters and brought us here on holidays to visit our mum and dad. Since we were Catholics there were no jobs to be had in Northern Ireland. The jobs went to the Protestants. So my folks had to come south of the border, to the Republic, if their little ones were to eat."

"Am I going to see your family?" Susy asked.

"If my family will see me," Liam replied mysteriously. "That, my love, is what we have to talk about. Let's order first."

They were well into a grand dinner of fresh salmon, caught from the nearby river, when Liam O'Toole told Susy the story.

He had grown up in the Falls Road area of Catholic Belfast, and his family had known nothing but the poverty that was the typical lot of anyone not born Protestant in English Ireland. When he was ten, his father died from a sniper's bullet while out for a Sunday stroll, leaving his mother with eight children— Liam was the eldest—and no income.

To support the family, she worked herself to the bone at nights as a charwoman at British army headquarters. Sometimes she took young O'Toole with her to help out. By the time he was thirteen, Liam went to school by day and worked with his mother until the wee hours of the morning, cleaning toilets and scrubbing floors for the soldiers who occupied their city.

Liam O'Toole had been brought up an Irish nationalist. There was little choice for Catholics in the six counties controlled by Britain. But from an early age his father had always taught him to fight in honorable ways. To his father, there was nothing honorable about the Irish Republican Army.

Thirteen-year-old boys don't see it that way, though. The local hero was a fellow named Tom Murphy, the legendary commander of the Belfast IRA. No one knew what he looked like, and no one knew where he was; Tom Murphy had long gone underground.

There were stories, though. Someone had seen him once, or met him. Or during one of the frequent riots, a man would appear and lend a helping hand to some demonstrator mowed down by a British bullet or run down by a police horse. Afterward they'd say it was Tom Murphy himself who had been there to save the day. Like all typical thirteen-year-old boys, Liam

O'Toole was in love with his hero and wanted to grow up to be just like him.

One night his mother was sick with one of her frequent chest ailments, and young O'Toole went off by himself to do the work at British army headquarters. Hours later, as he struggled home through the cold, wet streets of winter Belfast, laden with mops and buckets from the awful work, he saw a tall, handsome man standing in the darkness against a brick wall. The streetlights had been knocked out months earlier in a riot. For a moment young Liam was frightened. Then the man spoke.

"Barely a boy, but more than a man's job, isn't it, Liam O'Toole? Taking care of your poor widowed mother?"

Curiosity about this stranger who knew his name and seemed to know his family conquered his wariness. The man walked forward and extended his right hand.

"Tom Murphy. Pleased to be your friend."

In his surprise and confusion, and in his haste to shake the proffered hand, Liam dropped the load of buckets and mops. They fell to the sidewalk with a loud crash that resounded in the dark, sinister street. The stranger laughed and helped him pick them up.

"Let's walk," Tom Murphy suggested. "I'll help you home, buddy."

The teenage boy was too stunned to talk as they headed down the narrow grimy street toward the crumbling brick tenement where the O'Toole family lived. But it mattered little, since Tom Murphy had a lot to say.

He talked about Liam's work at the army headquarters, asking him what rooms he worked in, what he saw there, how many soldiers were around, what the security was like. It wasn't until the teenager had answered Murphy's questions that he began to realize why they were being asked.

Finally they reached the doorstep of Liam's house.

"Just between us, buddy. Our secret. Okay?" Murphy said. "We're in this together, you and I. Those bastards killed your father."

"A-All right," Liam stammered.

"Promise? Soldier's honor?" Tom Murphy raised his hand in a salute.

Liam O'Toole felt exhilarated. Not only had he just met the man who was the hero of every teenage Catholic boy, but the two of them were entering into a secret pact, a pact of honor.

"Promise," he said, proudly. He imitated Murphy and saluted back.

Murphy put his hands on young Liam's shoulders. "Good," he said, smiling. "You'll make a regular young soldier for the Irish Republican Army, Liam O'Toole. You'll do us proud! I'll be seeing you again."

It wasn't until Tom Murphy had said the words that Liam O'Toole realized that working for Tom Murphy meant working for the IRA. In a sudden panic of stricken conscience, he turned sharply and looked at the door of his mother's house, as if he were afraid she might be there listening to the conversation and disapproving of every word.

He caught his breath. No one was there.

He turned back to look at Tom Murphy again, ready to voice his sudden reservations.

The street was empty.

It wasn't until several months later that Tom Murphy made his second appearance. He seemed always to know exactly when Mrs. O'Toole was ill and when Liam had to go alone to do the cleaning work for the army. Again Murphy helped the teenager home with his buckets and brooms, and again they talked. This time Tom Murphy told young O'Toole about the struggle of the Irish against the English to gain mastery of their own fate in their own land. He told Liam things the boy already knew—about how Catholics never had jobs because the Protestants kept all the jobs for themselves, and about how the Royal Ulster Constabulary were a band of thugs who hated the Catholics and liked nothing better than to beat the living bejesus out of a good true Irishman. He talked about how Liam's father had been murdered by one of these thugs and how the culprit had never been found because the Royal Ulster Constabulary were hardly going to arrest one of their own.

These things Liam O'Toole already knew, but somehow the way Tom Murphy talked about them was different. The injustice seemed clearer. And when Tom Murphy talked about Ireland and the Irish, of the heroic kings of old and the centuries-long battle against the English overlords, young O'Toole was filled with pride and anger.

From time to time over a period of many months, Tom Murphy appeared for their secret meetings. For the most part he just talked. Sometimes he asked Liam

O'Toole more questions about British army headquarters. Finally he asked Liam for a special favor. He
needed some documents. He described them and told
Liam where they could be found—in a filing cabinet
in a certain office. Would Liam help the cause of Irish
freedom and get these papers for his old friend Tom
Murphy?

"But the filing cabinets are locked," Liam said. He
wanted to do it, wanted desperately to help his friend
and hero, to be a hero himself. But for some reason
that he could not explain, something to do with his
mother's telling him to be an honest man, he was
stalling.

Tom Murphy handed him a little key.

"That'll get you in there, my lad, or my name isn't
Tom Murphy." The IRA leader disappeared in the
Belfast night, leaving Liam O'Toole alone with his se-
cret.

He got the documents. It was so easy that even Liam
O'Toole was surprised. But now the boy was hooked.
A few weeks later Tom Murphy asked him for some-
thing else.

By the time a year had passed, Liam was an expert.
And within two years, Tom Murphy didn't have to ask
for things. O'Toole knew what to look for on his own.

Finally, one night when O'Toole was walking home
alone with the latest bundle of stolen papers stuffed in
his jacket, Tom Murphy wasn't waiting in his usual
place.

For a moment Liam was worried. Then he heard the
rattling engine of one of Belfast's big black taxis as the
vehicle slowed to a halt behind him. He turned

around. The window opened and the friendly smiling face of Tom Murphy appeared. The door opened, and Murphy beckoned him inside.

There were two other men in the taxi. As they hurtled off through the streets toward the edge of the city, Murphy introduced him.

"This is my good buddy, Liam O'Toole, boys. And never a braver lad have you met." Murphy turned to Liam. "Liam, tonight is a night you'll remember for the rest of your life."

It was. It was the night he was officially inducted into the Irish Republican Army. The secret ceremony took place in a four-hundred-year-old stone farmhouse in the countryside. They took him back to Belfast in the early hours of the morning as the fresh light of dawn broke over the city. Liam O'Toole, fourteen going on fifteen, felt as if it were the first morning of his life. As he left the car, Tom Murphy slapped him on the back.

"You're a man now, Liam. You're one of us."

And as he walked the rest of the distance home, Liam O'Toole reflected on some of the things he'd been told during the secret ceremony. There was no backing out. Stool pigeons, cowards, traitors and quitters met a similar fate. Death.

But the possibility that harsh IRA punishment would ever be applied to him was far from his thoughts as he opened the door to his mother's house. He felt like a man. He was proud to have sworn the oath of a soldier in the Irish Republican Army. As a soldier, he would dedicate his life to fighting the English. Or he would die, accepting martyrdom in the cause of Irish freedom.

In the next few years, Liam O'Toole learned much. He learned that at night while working with his mother at British army headquarters, he could easily slip away for a few moments. The entrance to the munitions stores was scarcely guarded. He learned to open locks without keys, and he learned that ammunition, small arms and, in particular, small quantities of explosives and some of the smaller mortars could easily be smuggled out in his bulky jacket or inside his pant legs.

At the secret meetings in the country, Liam learned how to assemble the hardware he stole into bombs. For three years O'Toole thought that he alone of all his friends was a member of the IRA. He kept his secret well. But at one of their meetings, he met another teenager, whom he knew from the Falls Road neighborhood. He and Seamus Killerbey became fast friends and quickly acquired a reputation in Catholic Belfast as a fierce team when it came to manning the barricades during riots against the British.

One day, the word was passed to him that Tom Murphy and the other commanders of the Provos— the provisional wing of the IRA—wanted to see him. He kept the secret rendezvous, and they gave him specific orders. His reputation as a street fighter and militant Irish nationalist was growing. It was only a matter of time before it came to the attention of the British authorities, before the connection was made to the O'Tooles who cleaned the headquarters, and they lost their jobs and came under investigation. Therefore, he was told, it was time to act.

Tom Murphy handed him a package. Liam knew it was a bomb.

"Since we won't have access to the munitions anymore," Murphy said, smiling grimly, "you might as well blow them up."

That night Liam's mother was sick again. Liam was preparing to go off alone, when Ellen Lorraine, a sister who was two years younger, appeared at the door in her working clothes and jacket.

"Mother says I'm to go and help you out, says you're dragging yourself about these days and your school's not up to much, and if I go we'll get it done twice as fast."

Liam was afraid to protest, afraid to draw suspicion. They finished their work at headquarters, and Liam quietly slipped away and set the bomb. He gave it an hour on the fuse. He had become such an expert at it, he knew after that the mistake wasn't his.

A few minutes later, Liam and his sister left the compound, loaded up with their equipment, and started home. Ellen Lorraine announced she'd left her book bag and had to go back.

It was as if he saw the danger with a kind of second sight.

"No, leave it, Ellen. I'll pick it up tomorrow."

Ellen Lorraine insisted, despite Liam's repeated protestations.

Liam waited impatiently outside the gates as she went back through security. The explosion came two minutes later. It destroyed British army headquarters, killing twenty-three soldiers. Ellen Lorraine was dragged from the ruins more dead than alive. Eventually she recovered, although she would be horribly disfigured for life.

For the IRA all hell broke loose.

The reprisals included mass arrests of hundreds of men and women. Liam was among them. Sean Killerbey was, also. It was said that the British wouldn't stop until they tracked down Tom Murphy, put him up against a wall and shot him.

O'Toole was held for a week of intensive questioning, during which he was repeatedly beaten. But the seventeen-year-old honored his oath. Not a single incriminating word passed his lips.

The British had no evidence of his involvement. And the fact that his own sister had sustained injuries seemed to convince them that Liam couldn't have been involved in the terrorist bombing.

It wasn't until he got home that he realized he had a price yet to pay. When he walked in the door his mother nailed him with a hard look.

"Did you do it?" she asked.

He tried to hold her stare, but his eyes wavered with the guilt of lying.

"No."

She spun away from him.

"I have no son named Liam O'Toole."

"But . . ." Liam began to protest.

"I have no son." She spoke with her back turned to him. "No son named Liam O'Toole."

Nothing else needed to be said. He knew his mother would never forgive him. He was disowned.

He left the house, little knowing how many years and how many wars would pass before he could return.

3

O'Toole sat back, weary from the load of memories as he finished telling his story. Susy had put down her fork and folded her napkin on the table. Dinner was over.

"I went to America," he concluded. "Ran away to another country and promptly got involved in another war. Spent six years in Vietnam. That's where I met the Colonel. I was Barrabas's second in command over there. And in between battles there was always another broad and another bottle. Till I met you, Susy."

The corners of her luscious mouth turned up in a quick smile. "And your mother?"

"She's never forgiven and never forgotten. She still refuses to acknowledge me as her son. That's what I want to talk to you about, Susy. I've been thinking. Maybe you can help. I'm a rich man now. I have enough money to buy my mother a decent house in the country and get her out of that Belfast slum. And enough to pay for the best plastic surgery for my sister Ellen Lorraine. It was her face that . . ."

His voice faltered and broke. Susy reached across the table and took his hand in hers, stroking it softly. After a moment Liam continued.

"Maybe now, now that I'm with you and I've given up... fighting, maybe now I can get through to her. She's old. She hasn't got a lot of time left. I want to make it up to her before she goes. I was wondering... if you'd go see her, Susy. Tell her you're my wife. Maybe she'll listen to you...."

"Of course, Liam. I'll do anything to help you." She squeezed his hand gently. Toying with her spoon, she looked away. "Tom Murphy, your commander, your childhood hero—he was shot, wasn't he?"

O'Toole looked at her, a little surprised that she knew.

"My family's Irish, too, Liam. I remember hearing my folks talk about it years ago. I was a teenager then, too." She smiled.

Liam nodded. "The cell I belonged to went underground immediately after the trouble started, as I knew it would, and I never saw Tom Murphy again. But a few days after I left Belfast, the Brits raided the old stone farmhouse in the country where we had those meetings. They did exactly what it was rumored they would do. Shot him. Up against a wall. Of course they said he was trying to escape, that he was an armed fugitive."

"How did they find the house?"

O'Toole shrugged. "They arrested a lot of men. Someone talked, I guess. I was long gone, and I've had nothing more to do with the IRA since then. It's an ugly war that's being fought here, and I'm not convinced any longer that the IRA are in the right. I was young and impressionable then. Bloody stupid, actually. There's a time to fight and a time to die, for Ireland as much as for any other country or cause. But if a man's going to die for something, he's got to be damn sure of the company he keeps. For me, the IRA's not it.''

Susy nodded her understanding and smiled across the table at him.

"Let's go upstairs," Liam whispered across the table, a gleam in his eyes. "To bed."

They left the restaurant arm in arm and crossed into the grand, open foyer of the castle. A large party of German tourists had just arrived on a tour bus and had congregated near the front doors as their mountains of luggage were wheeled in. Suddenly Liam O'Toole froze in his tracks and stared at a man who was disappearing through the front doors.

"What's the matter, darling?" Susy asked.

O'Toole shook his head and snickered in spite of himself. "Nothing, I guess. No, nothing."

Liam saw the way she looked at him. He was learning quickly that he couldn't hide anything from her. "It's nothing, really. It's all that talk at dinner, I guess."

"What do you mean?" she asked, curious and concerned.

"Well," O'Toole said, slightly embarrassed, "that man who just walked outside. I could have sworn he was Seamus Killerbey, the man I was friends with in the IRA years ago."

"Do you think . . . ?"

O'Toole shook his head emphatically. "Just someone who looked a bit like him, I suppose." He put his arm around her shoulders again and drew her toward the grand staircase that led up to the suites. He pressed the soft curves of her against his body. "Let's forget about it. A little loving in the present should help to wipe out old hatreds." With a sweeping gesture at the staircase, he added, "After you, darlin'...."

SEVERAL THOUSAND KILOMETERS AWAY, the party in the Atlantic City luxury casino was in the twenty-fourth hour of its eighth day. On the first floor of the two-story penthouse suite several dozen men and women lurched in circles as they attempted to dance to the eight-piece orchestra's rendition of a moldy hit from years gone by.

A man in a wrinkled tuxedo wobbled on the circular staircase that led to the top floor. He had his arms around the waists of the two voluptuous babes beside him. They giggled and dug in their heels as he tried to persuade them to go up to one of the bedrooms.

"But I want to see Alex," one of them protested, whining and pouting.

"Me, too," the second echoed.

"Come on, girls," the man pleaded, slurring his words. "Alex is busy."

"Then I want to see Nate," the first one demanded.

"Me, too," the second one echoed.

"Nate's busy too, babe. Let's just go for a walk upstairs and I'll show you the circular bed. It rotates."

Upstairs in the large master bedroom the circular bed was indeed rotating.

Alex Nanos and Nate Beck sat back comfortably in leather sling chairs, watching it go around. Aboard the bed, six of the most curvaceous examples of Atlantic City flesh undulated, vaguely in time with the music from below. The bed was a lazy Susan of lascivious morsels, each hoping her performance would win her the title as main course. As the gyrating women swung past the two vacationing mercenary soldiers they winked, the gleam in their eyes inspired by the money that had been flowing freely from the two soldiers' pockets for the past week or so.

"Ain't it the life, Nate?" Alex said, sighing. "I like this one coming round now. The one with the perky nips. Ain't it the life, Nate?"

Nate Beck's eyes passed over the nips and flowed down toward the flanks. They checked out all right, but this one wasn't as long legged as the blonde whose turn was coming up.

"Which one?" Nanos sighed again, his dreamlike eyes gazing after the one with the nips.

"Which what?" Nate asked.

Alex looked at his old buddy with exasperation. "Which one do you want tonight?"

"Oh." Nate smiled. It was like being in a Roman slave market or something. "This one," he said as the long, slender flanks came into view.

The sound of shattering glass burst through the music from downstairs. It was loud. It sounded like a lot of glass. The two mercs looked at each other. Alex shrugged. Nate shrugged. They went back to looking at the revolving display in front of them.

They were interrupted again by a bloodcurdling scream. It was a woman's scream. Definitely female. And whoever she was she made it sound like a matter of life or death. The screaming was soon followed by panicked shrieks. Also female.

"'Scuse us," Nanos said to the maidens, rising from his chair. "We'll be right back."

Nate Beck stood and followed Alex Nanos to the door. He looked back before he went through it. "Keep dancing," he told them. None of them seemed to have noticed the audience's departure.

The two men made their way to the staircase. The orchestra had stopped playing, and the various band members were staring, openmouthed, at the enormous, shattered, twenty-foot-high glass windows that looked out over the Atlantic Ocean.

The couples who, a few minutes earlier, had been dancing, now stood aside, watching as the man in the rumpled tuxedo threw a shrieking young woman over his shoulder. She kicked, screamed and clawed at his back as he walked toward the broken window. Cold spring winds blew into the hotel suite. There was a thirty-story drop from the window to the oceanside drive below. There was no balcony. And the desperate screams came from outside.

As Nanos and Beck came downstairs, they could see white hands clinging desperately to the narrow ledge outside the window.

"Shit," Alex Nanos muttered. "Who the fuck are all these people, anyway?"

"You invited them. Some of them. From the casino, after you won all that money."

"Shit, yeah." The vaguest recollection of it came back. He had won big about a week before. The winning streak had lasted for hours, and when he had finally called it quits, he was richer by a hundred thousand dollars of the Flamingo Lounge's money. The scowls of the stiff-suited managers followed him from the room. That was when the party had started.

Another bone-chilling scream filled the room, and the two white hands on the ledge outside slipped closer to no return.

"I knew they would get us in trouble!" Nate Beck wailed, a full load of good Jewish guilt dropping on him like a two-ton weight. It always happened to him when pleasure resulted in crisis, and when he partied with Alex Nanos, crisis was usually high on the agenda.

Nanos was more businesslike. He walked swiftly to the man in the rumpled tuxedo just as he was hoisting the young woman from his shoulder and preparing to throw her through the broken window. Nanos grabbed the terrified creature's belt as she hit the top of the arc, and with his powerful left arm he held her suspended in midair. With his right arm he reached back and slugged the man in the tuxedo as hard as he could, full in the face. For a split second the man looked surprised. Then blood gushed from his nose, down the front of his white shirt; his eyes rolled up and he fell over, unconscious.

Nanos dropped the girl and moved to the window. Nate Beck was already there. The mercs reached down, each grabbing a slender wrist just as the hands let go of the thin ledge. They hoisted her up over the edge. Her face was white with terror. She looked at each of her rescuers and promptly passed out.

"You take her," Alex told Nate, lifting her limp body up and laying it across Beck's shoulder. "I'll tend to the asshole." He pointed to the unconscious man in the tuxedo.

"They get so upset when they can't get laid," Nate Beck muttered, turning past the crowd of awed, speechless party goers and headed toward the staircase. "I'll put her in the shower."

Nanos ripped a lamp from the wall and tore the electric cord from its base. Quickly he tied it in a harness around the unconscious man in the tuxedo. He ripped out another electric lamp cord and ran it from the harness to the wrought-iron banister. Then he lowered the man out the hole in the window, leaving him suspended thirty stories above nothing.

"I hate assholes," he muttered when he had finished. He looked around. The people he had invited to his party didn't seem to care. The musicians in the band looked as though they were on the verge of collapse. He dug into his pocket and pulled out a wad of money, and started to count it.

"Fuck it," he said to himself. There was too much. And it was only a small fraction of the loose cash left over from his winnings. He walked across to the petrified bandleader and shoved the money into his hand. "Play it again, Sam," he ordered. Then he turned to the crowd. "Get out the booze and let's keep dancing!"

They cheered, a few of them casting guilty looks at the electric cords that ran out the broken window. Someone was going to wake up in a nightmare, Nanos thought, heading for the stairs and the flesh-a-rama on the rotating circular bed.

Nate Beck was back in position in the leather sling chair when Nanos walked in. The six ladies still undulated, as if nothing had happened. The bathroom door was closed, but Alex could hear the steady sound of the shower and muffled sobs from within.

"Y'know, I'll think I'll take the one with the flanks," Nate Beck said as Alex took his seat and the beauty sailed past.

"Ain't it the life?" Alex said.

"Yeah. Just think of what poor old Liam is missing." Nate's voice sounded wistful.

"Yeah."

The two bachelor mercs stared at the bevy of beauties.

"I still can't believe he's turned in his traveling card," Nanos said sadly, referring to O'Toole's resignation from the team of hard-fighting soldiers who worked for Nile Barrabas.

"Yeah."

The telephone rang. Nanos reached out and answered it. He listened without speaking, then hung up.

"Who was that?"

"The management."

"Oh."

The bed of babes kept rotating. Nanos volunteered nothing further.

"What did they want?"

"Some guy's hanging from a broken window, screaming his lungs out."

"Oh."

Beck could make out some terrified shrieks for help from far away. They were almost drowned out by the music. The band played on.

"Let's phone him," Nanos suggested.

"Who?"

"O'Toole."

"He's on his honeymoon."

"I know that," Nanos said indignantly. He reached for the telephone. "Let's phone and say hello."

"Where is he?"

"With Susy."

Beck rolled his eyes. "You're kidding. What a great idea. Imagine, a honeymoon with your wife. It's inspired."

"He's at some castle in Ireland. I got the phone number here somewhere." He rifled his pockets and came up with a slip of paper with some numbers scrawled on it. "I don't believe he's really quit the SOBs." Nanos started dialing.

"What're you going to tell him?" Beck asked, doubtful of the wisdom of interrupting Liam O'Toole's long-delayed honeymoon.

Nanos paused and thought for a moment. "Come home. All is forgiven?" He shrugged.

Beck looked at Nanos and shrugged back. "Sure," he said, still doubtful. "Why not."

MOONLIGHT FILTERED IN through the high casement window and wavered on the bed, diffused through the windblown curtains.

For the first few moments Liam O'Toole had some performance anxiety. His conversation with Susy had ripped open his past like a bloody wound. But as they came together the ghosts evaporated, and he felt himself once again captivated by the present, grateful for the future. Their heat become overpowering as they rocked together. The past, the present, all of it vanished in the intensity.

On the verge of climax, somewhere in the recesses of his consciousness Liam O'Toole registered movement in the room. Wave after wave of pleasure rippled through him, pushing the awareness aside.

A light went on.

O'Toole blinked. He froze. His eyes locked with Susy's. For a brief moment he saw fear there. Fear and something else. Before he could read it, a hard voice shouted an order.

He felt rough hands on his body, pulling him from the bed. He reacted like a soldier. His leg curled forward and struck solidly back. It hit something. He heard a man yelp with pain. With a powerful concentration of energy, he struck up with one of his elbows, again meeting flesh, and twisted.

He came around to face a man with thick black hair. Another man was behind him, recovering from the kick in the groin. In the darkness he could see other shapes, other men moving toward the bed.

The phone started to ring.

O'Toole balled his fist and struck savagely at the man in front of him, knocking him back. Quickly he brought his knee up, and it connected with his opponent's solar plexus. A third man reached the bed. But this time O'Toole was on his feet. He grabbed a lamp from the bedside table and swung it hard at the man's head. The bulb shattered, and the man shrieked as broken glass split open his face. O'Toole swung again, hard, and felt the base of the lamp crush bone. The man dropped to the floor.

The other two thugs had recovered from their blows and were making a grab for him. Two more were coming from across the room. O'Toole thought of only one thing: Susy. He had to protect her. He backed toward the bed, searching for a weapon.

The phone rang again.

He grabbed it. The receiver fell off and clunked on the floor. Holding the rest of the phone tightly in his hand, he powered it into the face of the man in front of him. The attacker dropped like a stone.

Before O'Toole could react again, hands grabbed his arms and his neck. He could see a hand raised, with something in it. A blackjack. Then he saw the face. For a second he thought it must be a dream, and he tried to wake up. The face belonged to Seamus Killerbey. The blackjack swung toward his temple.

A solid force crashed against the side of his head, cloaking his view of the face in a shower of stars. The stars faded like fireworks.

They were replaced by blackness.

IN THE LUXURY PENTHOUSE SUITE in Atlantic City, Alex Nanos stared at the telephone receiver in his hand.

"What's happening?" Nate Beck asked, seeing Alex's puzzlement.

"Beats me." Alex told him what he had heard. "What do you think's going on?"

Nanos shrugged. Then he smiled conspiratorially and shook his head. "Sounds like one helluva honeymoon."

Nate Beck nodded.

Alex slapped his friend on the shoulder. "You want the one with the flanks," he said, jerking his head toward the fantasy figures still sliding by on the rotating bed. "I'll take the one with the nips." He managed a smile.

4

Billy Starfoot II—Billy Two, to his fellow SOBs—winced against the bright Arizona-desert sunlight and brushed his hand along his forehead. He felt woozy again. He doubted it was the heat. A full-blooded Osage, he had grown up on this kind of land and was more acclimatized to it than to the cold wet north. But the dizzy spells had begun half an hour earlier, when he arrived at the Navaho village, and were growing stronger and more frequent.

Standing about two heads below his six-foot frame, old Mrs. Cawtooth, layered against the heat under a mound of blankets woven in geometric designs, looked up at him tearfully.

"It is the land of my father, and my father's father, and his father. Their spirits reside here. What will become of these spirits if we are forced to move? They will wander alone in the desert. They will become angered if we abandon them. And then who knows what will become of the land. Terrible things happen when the spirits are angry. And how will we fare if we are forced to go elsewhere? How can we take the spirits with us, when they are rooted to the land that holds their bones? We will be denied the protection of our forebears.''

Great thick tears rolled down the old woman's wizened cheeks. A recent government tribunal had decided that thousands of acres of Navaho ancestral land in fact belonged to the neighboring Hopi Indians, and had ordered the third and fourth generations of wandering Navahos to move elsewhere. As Billy knew, for the Indians, much more was at stake than a few acres of barren grazing land for sheep. If the Navahos were forced to move, they would be abandoning the spirits of their ancestors, who had lived on the land before them. The old people would die in their new homes. The young people, uprooted and drifting, would gravitate toward the big cities.

Billy Two had spent weeks traveling the halls of Washington's bureaucracies, trying to explain this. He felt a deep commitment to work for the betterment of the native peoples of America—especially since his own Osage family had been particularly rapacious after the discovery of oil under their Oklahoma reservation. But this time it looked as though his mission would end in failure. The government officials were intractable. He had returned to Arizona defeated, to tell these people they had no choice.

He grasped the old woman firmly by her stout shoulders and looked directly into her big wet eyes. ''Mrs. Cawtooth, I understand. I promise you I will do everything I can. But right now the government man says you must move in two months' time. I will keep trying. I promise.'' He shook his head, fighting another dizzy spell. "Now I must go back to talk to the government again. I will return. I promise."

With that, Billy Two turned and headed for the tawny Ford station wagon parked at the side of the highway. By the time he reached the door, his head was swimming in a kaleidoscope of exploding colors. He crashed into the front seat as his legs buckled under him. "What the hell..." he muttered. A voice answered him, a voice that was as soft as a hot wind fluttering along the cactus forests of the high desert. It spoke no words, but it soothed him. He felt a babble of whispers at his ears, as if he were being told a dozen secrets at the same time and could not make out a single one of them.

He had heard this voice before. It had come to him while he'd been strapped down on a torture table at a so-called psychiatric clinic in Moscow, with sulfazine burning through his body. That was the first time Hawk Spirit, the warrior god of the Osage people, had spoken to him. It had happened on several occasions since.

He recalled how, at those times, he had felt he was moving through a dream. He could not explain how or why he did what he did. Sometimes it was the right thing—aiming a weapon in darkness and scoring a bull's-eye in time to save the life of one of his comrades; knowing exactly where an enemy was about to come from. Those times his buddies congratulated him for what they called his "sixth sense."

Other times, though, he found himself possessed by strange compulsions—to run about in the midst of battle naked as a jaybird as his warrior ancestors once

had, to bay like a coyote at the full moon after a score
had been settled and the bodies of the enemy dead
gushed red lifeblood into the soil that reclaimed them.
Those times the Soldiers of Barrabas looked at him as
if he were crazy. As if he were dangerous.

How could he explain it to them? Hawk Spirit?
They'd think he was nuts. They would say that the
Spetsnaz were responsible, that the Russian military
police had tortured the sanity right out of him.

This time, however, the voice came to him like in-
terference on a radio dial at night when too many sta-
tions crowded the airways and not one could be dialed
in properly. He tried to focus, to listen through the
whispering chatter to hear something he could understand.

Suddenly, under his closed lids, an image jerked vi-
olently into his eyes. First he saw a landscape of green
rolling fields leading to low craggy mountains. Then,
like a newsreel gone wild, an enormous diesel train
smashed through his head as if he were standing in
front of it.

For a moment the image went fuzzy, like a television set on the blink. Then it went dark. Picture tube
blown? he thought. Gradually light returned. He was
in a small dark room with stone walls. He was being
beaten savagely about the face. He tried to stop the
assault, but he couldn't move.... The screen went dead
again.

He heard the voices whispering in his ears. He
thought one was struggling to be heard above the others, but it was being drowned out. Excruciating pain
flashed through the front of his skull, followed by an

explosion of color. For a second, barely long enough to comprehend it, he saw an image. His breath caught in his throat. Abruptly the image flashed out and the voices stopped.

He opened his eyes. He was sitting in the front seat of his station wagon on an Arizona highway. The keys were in the ignition, and the car's engine purred. He didn't remember starting it.

The dizziness he felt earlier was gone now, and the sharp pain had been replaced by a low, dull ache, scarcely noticeable. He felt the skin on the side of his face stinging, and when he looked into the rearview mirror, he saw a livid mark, quickly shading into a bruise.

The spirits of this land are angry spirits, he thought. So angry, that when Hawk Spirit had come to him, the ancestral Navaho spirits had crowded in on his wavelength in protest. That's what had made this message so difficult, and so painful.

But it was the last vivid image that had flashed before his eyes that sat like an iron lump in the pit of his stomach. Six of the seven Soldiers of Barrabas stood together. One was missing, but he couldn't tell who. The others stood in a growing pool of thick red blood.

Billy Two jerked the station wagon into gear. His foot sank on the accelerator. As far as he was concerned, there was only one thing to do. See Barrabas. Where the visions ended, logic began.

IN NEW YORK CITY, Walker Jessup, a.k.a. the Fixer, casually surveyed the view through the plate-glass windows of his sixtieth-floor office. The cold spring rain had turned the tall towers of Manhattan a gloomy gray, and although it was morning, the building burned through the drizzle with the office lights of millions of toiling workers. He walked to the Telex machine and ripped off the long yellow sheet with the latest Interpol data.

He scanned the sheet quickly as he returned to his desk and sank his mammoth frame into the high-backed, soft-cushioned swivel chair. Must lose weight, he thought to himself for the umpteenth time that day. He had the same thought many times every day. Each time it was followed by a mental shrug—it's the thought that counts.

Walker Jessup had once been one of the CIA's top operatives. Some years ago, he had put aside his career on the wild side of danger and taken up a cushier posting in private business. With the contacts he had made over a fifteen-year career as an intelligence agent, he became indispensable as a broker in the world of espionage and government intrigue.

If the cash was sufficient, no job was too big for Walker Jessup. At any given time the Fixer had a piece of the action in any one of a dozen Third World brushfires, coups d'état and assorted other sordid affairs. He was the only contact between the secret House committee and the covert action team led by ex-Vietnam veteran Colonel Nile Barrabas.

Ostensibly, Barrabas and his team of eccentric professional men—and woman—worked privately for Walker Jessup. In reality, the team had been put together solely for the use of the American government. Any job too dirty for Washington or its various agencies to handle was theirs.

There was no shortage of work.

As Jessup read over the morning's Interpol list, a humdrum part of the daily office routine, he silently filed away various details in his prodigious memory for future reference. Today it was the usual. Another car-bomb suicide in Beirut meant one less maniac to worry about. More executions in Iran. Another East German spy had been uncovered in the West German premier's office, but that was hardly news. Unidentified spy planes had been sighted over Burma. An environmentalist's yacht was blown up in a New Zealand harbor. An American tourist and his wife had been kidnapped by the IRA from an Irish hotel; their identities had not yet been established.

The usual.

Walker Jessup felt familiar rumblings in his stomach. He picked up the telephone and made a reservation for lunch—without reservations. After all, it was the thought that counted.

5

Consciousness returned painfully. He was dimly aware of being somewhere he didn't want to be. It was cold. He shivered. His hands were tied behind his back. Something hard was stuck between his back and his arms. A chair. The back of a chair. He was tied, sitting up, in a wooden chair. It was very cold. Feeling ended at his wrists and his ankles.

With an immense effort he lifted his head and tried to open his eyes. His eyes were already open. He was in pitch blackness. The side of his face felt raw. With the tip of his tongue he checked his molars. One was loose. He tasted blood and spat. He noticed a thin line of light in the darkness. A door, he thought. But it was impossible to tell how far away it was.

He had no sense of how long he'd been there. He drifted in and out of consciousness. His stomach felt like a cesspool and most of the time he wanted to puke. Nothing came up. He dry-heaved. His throat was swollen and raw. He thought of Susy.

He was half asleep, when he heard a whining creak and looked up to see the door open. The tall figure of a man filled the frame. For a moment the man watched him. Then he turned away.

"He's awake, boys. Someone tell the commander."

A few moments later another figure filled the doorway—a bigger, taller one. The man reached out, and suddenly the lights went on.

Pain seared through his eyes and he shut them, then forced them open against the tears and the harsh light. He had one thought now. He wanted another look at the man in the doorway.

A deep rich voice, thick with brogue, boomed, "We meet again, Liam O'Toole."

O'Toole had his second look. His captor had grown from a boy into a big barrel-chested man with thick-muscled arms. His face was handsome, his lips thick and his fair skin framed by a mop of unruly, sandy hair. It had been many years, many miles and many wars since they had seen each other. But there was no mistaking O'Toole's teenage buddy, Seamus Killerbey.

Tense with hatred and anger, O'Toole looked at the IRA commander. "Where's Susy?" he snarled. "Where is she?"

Killerbey smiled. "We'll get to that." He walked several steps into the room. Behind him, other men crowded the doorway. They were young, barely out of their teens, and they carried small submachine guns, which O'Toole recognized as MAC-10s.

For the first time, O'Toole began to take details of his surroundings. They weren't many. The floor was packed earth, and the walls were wet stone. He recognized the place to be a cellar in an old house, probably in the country.

Killerbey circled the bound prisoner slowly. O'Toole resisted the temptation to look at him. Livid, desperate, he strained against the thick rope that held his arms and legs to the wooden chair.

"Long time no see. Isn't that what you Americans say?" Killerbey joked, faking an American accent. He came around in front of O'Toole again. "You are an American now, aren't you, Liam? Turned your back on your homeland, did you?"

"What do you want?"

"Nothing now." Killerbey bent down to stare into O'Toole's face. "Now that I've got you."

"My wife. Where is she?"

"I said we'd get to that."

O'Toole reacted. His instincts told him to slug the bastard in the face. But when his arm tried to fly up, the bonds around his wrists held. The chair rocked forward, almost tipping.

Killerbey jumped back, startled. Then he laughed to cover his surprise. "Ha-ha. Little edgy there, O'Toole? We've some talking to do."

O'Toole trembled silently, his lips pressed tightly together as he suppressed his rage.

Killerbey continued, eyeing his prisoner as he talked. "You are now a prisoner of the Irish Republican Army. You are being held pending your trial before a military tribunal. The members of the tribunal will hear the charges, determine their merit and pronounce judgment. If you are guilty, you will be sentenced."

O'Toole looked at him in disbelief. "What in hell are you talking about, Seamus?"

"Don't pretend you don't know, Liam. Remember the vows we made, years ago now. We swore never to betray Ireland."

"And I never have, Seamus. I went to America just like a million other Irish before me. That's no crime—unless maybe you're in Iran."

"That's not what I'm talking about, Liam. The charge against you is treason. You will be tried for the murder of a man whose memory cries out for justice."

"Wha—"

"Thomas Murphy!"

O'Toole looked at Seamus Killerbey, speechless. He wondered if the Irishman was stark, raving mad. Behind him, at the doorway, the other young men looked on, a mixture of curiosity and contempt on their faces.

"Tom Murphy?" O'Toole said finally. "The murder of Tom Murphy?"

"That's right, Liam. Everyone knows someone betrayed him to the British, told them where to find him. And find him they did, and shot him down like a dog. And the betrayer, Liam O'Toole, was you."

Killerbey's cold blue eyes glinted as he spoke. O'Toole watched him. He decided that the eyes were deadly. The Seamus Killerbey he had known as a teenager had been much like himself—full of juice, and a little gullible, easily impressed and too eager to save Ireland single-handedly. But Killerbey had become a man and now he was a killer.

"I was long gone, Seamus. I was in America by the time they found Murphy."

"You will have time to answer to the charges against you, Liam. But not now."

"All I want now is my wife, Seamus. Where is she?"

A strange smile crossed the IRA commander's face, and his eyes carried a message O'Toole could not read.

"We'll get to that in a minute, Liam. I'm not finished discussing this with you yet. You will be put on trial and allowed to testify on your own behalf. You will not be allowed to call witnesses to testify in your favor. You will not be allowed to cross-examine witnesses testifying against you. You are guilty until you prove yourself innocent."

Seamus Killerbey stopped and stared at his prisoner, waiting for a reaction. O'Toole sat perfectly still. He knew from the way his captor was talking that he was getting around to something. A deal with the Devil, O'Toole thought.

"But there's a way out. A way you can prove your loyalty to Ireland. And perhaps—I don't promise—the charges against you will be found unsubstantiated."

O'Toole looked at Seamus Killerbey with doubt in his eyes. "What's that, Killerbey?" he asked, going for broke.

"We need an expert on demolitions," Killerbey said, getting straight to the point. "We have a project in mind, and we need someone to set up equipment for it." He smiled generously.

O'Toole stared at the IRA commander with cold loathing. "You know something, Seamus? When the Devil's dealing, no one gets a winning hand."

Killerbey's smile faded. He looked at O'Toole sadly. "Is that your answer, Liam?"

"The answer's no, Seamus. No. Don't ask me to be a part of your ritual bloodbaths. That's why I went to America after the troubles a long time ago."

Killerbey pulled a knife from the sheath at his waist and turned to the men at the doorway. "Davy!" he shouted to one young man with dark curly hair and a pug nose. Davy disappeared for a moment. When he returned he handed something to Killerbey, who took it from him on the point of his knife.

O'Toole recognized it immediately. He felt the cold teeth of fear bite through him. It was a brassiere. It was Susy's. It had been cut off her body.

"You asked about your wife, Liam." Killerbey tossed the brassiere at O'Toole. It hit him in the face and fell onto the floor. "The next thing we bring you will be her panties. But those will be covered with blood. Now, do you agree to do it for us or not?"

The prisoner closed his eyes and his head fell. One word, her name, rang in his mind, and with it the image of her face. He felt his heart racing, felt the deadness in the pit of his stomach. He had no choice.

"Do you?" Killerbey's unrelenting voice demanded again.

Without raising his eyes, O'Toole nodded.

"Say it!" Killerbey ordered.

The prisoner sighed wearily. "Yes." His voice was low.

The IRA commander turned to the men at the doorway. "Okay, boys, fix him up. Feed him and clean him, and when he's rested bring him to me."

As Seamus Killerbey backed out of the room the men walked forward. They quickly began to undo the ropes around O'Toole's wrists and ankles. He felt an agonizing pain in his hands and feet as the blood started to pound into the numbed extremities.

Killerbey stopped at the doorway and turned back. "By the way, Liam. I almost forgot." He smiled grandly when their eyes met. "Welcome home."

THE NEXT DAY Liam O'Toole was awakened early. After the encounter with Killerbey, he had been taken upstairs and locked in a small bedroom. There was a basin of warm water and a tray of food. He washed himself and ate, feeling the nourishment rejuvenate him. In the reflection in the basin of water he saw that his face was a mess. His lips were cut and sore, and a big raw bruise covered one side of his face.

When his energy returned, he searched the room for a means of escape, but the old Irish farmhouse, built to withstand the cold strong winds of the Irish Sea and the ravages of centuries, made a fine stone prison. The window was probably too small to climb out of—in any case it was stoutly shuttered with thick, iron-reinforced wood. The door was the same.

For a long time he lay restless on the cot, trying to make some sense of the events that had led up to this predicament. Eventually he slept.

His guess that he was in a farmhouse was confirmed when the guards led him outside. It was a glorious Irish morning. There was a cool wet chill in the air, the sky was blue and the rolling fields that stretched away to low craggy mountains shone green. He recognized the landscape. He was in County Armagh, south of Belfast, one of the six counties of

Northern Ireland. The guards led him silently to a large outbuilding that had once been a barn.

When they pushed him through a small side door, he saw immediately that it was a machine shop. A big milk truck, partially dismantled, took up most of the room in the center of the barn. Opened crates along the sides revealed their contents: there were enough small mortars there to blow up Belfast.

Along one side, O'Toole noticed a half-dozen motorcycles, parked in a row. Seamus Killerbey was leaning over a fire-engine-red Norton, fitting a small homemade rocket launcher—they were called "mobile mines" by the IRA and "bombards" by the British army—under the gas tank. He stood up when O'Toole was brought in.

"We'll be smuggling them to Belfast this way," he told the Irish-American prisoner, smiling easily.

O'Toole grimaced. "I want to see Susy. How do I know she's still alive?"

The IRA commander kept smiling. "Now I figured you'd be asking that. And sure, it's a mite difficult for you to see her now, but speak to her you can surely do. And then we'll be having a bit of work for you, Liam O'Toole."

He motioned toward a telephone on a nearby workbench. "Put through a call to the house in New Jersey. You'll be assured that she couldn't be safer."

Surprised, O'Toole looked at Killerbey distrustfully.

"Go on," his captor ordered, jerking his head toward the telephone.

Reluctantly O'Toole picked up the receiver and dialed the international operator. He felt a cold steel gun barrel pressed into his neck and Seamus Killerbey's presence right behind him.

"And don't be getting any strange ideas about what to say along the way."

A minute later he heard the telephone ringing in Susy's suburban New Jersey house. It was answered on the third ring.

"Hello?" Susy's voice.

O'Toole's heart jumped, and he felt panic and relief simultaneously. She sounded worried.

"Susy. It's me."

"Liam! Where are you?"

O'Toole felt the gun barrel stab into his neck.

"I . . . I can't say. Are you all right?"

"Yes. Yes, I'm fine. But I've been worried sick about you. They took me directly to Shannon Airport and told me to return home. They said I'd hear from you. And they told me not to talk to anyone. They said they'd be watching me. Are you . . . ?"

"I'm all right, Susy."

"I want you, Liam. When are you coming home? What's going on? I don't understand."

"I can't tell you, Susy, I..." He felt the gun jab into him again. Killerbey moved around and motioned for him to hang up.

"I have to go, Susy. Just hang on. I'll be home soon."

Killerbey reached over and pushed the receiver cradle to disconnect the call.

"Our people on your side of the ocean report that she has stayed at home. As long as she does that, you'll be safe and she'll be safe. Now, Liam, to work. We have need of your expertise. We're starting our spring campaign, and we have a few projects on the go. The first one is the milk truck, Liam." Killerbey looked at the vehicle proudly. "We're going to blow a few people up with it."

THE PROJECT WAS SIMPLE but ingenious. Nine holes had been cut in the roof of the box van, and inside, instead of milk, nine homemade mortar launchers had been fixed in place. It was a bigger project than any the group had previously attempted. All O'Toole had to do was arrange the firing sequences and set up the remote-control device that would launch the deadly missiles from a distance. Killerbey supplied him with some figures involving distances in order for him to adjust the azimuth of the launchers.

O'Toole began work immediately, under the watchful eyes of three young guards. Under normal conditions he could have completed the job in a few hours. Instead he worked slowly, his mind racing feverishly, trying to think of a way out.

That afternoon Killerbey returned to the barn. He mounted one of the motorcycles and kick-started it. He walked it to the doorway, then shouted back at the guards. "No one rides the Red Devil except me." He pointed to the Norton, which had the bombards concealed under the gas tank. "I'll be back in two hours. Keep your eyes on him," he said, looking coldly at O'Toole. The prisoner appeared engrossed in the innards of the remote box. "'E's a tricky bastard." Then he revved the bike and roared off.

From the corner of his eye, O'Toole appraised the situation. There were three guards watching him now. They were bored and restless. There might be more at the house, but if there were, O'Toole hadn't seen them yet. For the time being, Susy was safe. If he made a successful break for it, he could make sure a friend of his got to Susy before a friend of Killerbey's did.

"Hey, Davy!" He shouted to the pug-nosed man who'd brought the brassiere to Killerbey the night before. "How 'bout some lunch?" He'd watched the guards chew on chocolate bars and potato chips all day, none of them showing any signs of having anything more substantial.

The three guards jumped at his voice. Davy looked to the other two for some sign of what to do. "Rion, Danny?" he asked them grudgingly.

Danny, a tall slim man with short brown hair, shrugged and looked at the third guard. "Sure, why not? Feed the guy. He's blowing up half of Ulster for us." Rion, a short dark man, laughed.

Davy shouldered his MAC-10 submachine gun and trotted off to the main house. Liam O'Toole worked on for a few minutes longer in silence, making minute adjustments to the remote box. By prying apart a couple of vital pins and leaving a frayed piece of wire touching a certain screw, he'd fixed it so that the remote would momentarily short circuit. The resulting power surge would change the wavelength of the signal. They'd never get the mortars off the ground. Or the milk truck, for that matter.

"Hey, fellows," O'Toole shouted over his shoulder when he was finished.

The two guards looked up from the girlie magazine that had been diverting their attention.

"Rion, Danny. I'll show you some adjustments I made to the mortars."

They looked at him suspiciously.

"Come here!" O'Toole sounded as innocent as possible.

The two guards trudged over to the back of the milk truck. They crowded beside him, one on each side.

"There now," O'Toole said, pointing at the dial on the cover as he finished screwing it on. He let go of it and jabbed hard out sideways with both elbows. He sank at the knees, giving the blows a sharp jolt upward.

Rion and Danny grunted and doubled over as the air was knocked out of them.

O'Toole didn't take time to notice.

He came up fast, throwing his weight into his left shoulder and Danny. His left arm came back hard. Danny lurched toward the floor. O'Toole slammed his left fist into Rion's pretty face. The IRA guard flipped backward. He flopped onto the floor, spread-eagled on his back. He raised his head weakly as the command to fight back went from brain to body. Body said no. Rion fell back, limp. He was out.

O'Toole was still busy.

Danny recovered his fall halfway down and grabbed a wrench from the worktable. He turned, swinging it at O'Toole.

The Irish-American moved in close, blocking high with his left forearm and ramming his knee up hard between Danny's legs.

Danny howled.

He dropped the pipe wrench.

O'Toole finished him off with two fists to the face.

Quickly he went to the large double doors at the front of the barn and peered out. Davy had just emerged from the door of the stone farmhouse and was making his way across the yard with a covered tray.

When he got to the barn door, he opened it with one hand, balancing the tray on the other, then closed the door behind him. He turned to face friends. He faced trouble, instead.

"I'll take that." O'Toole took the tray.

Whaap. Davy never saw what hit him.

Liam looked at the tray. Shit, he thought. I'm hungry. But there were too many other things to do.

Working frantically, he tied the three unconscious guards. As he did each of them, he was forced to keep watching the remaining ones, fearing they might come to. When he finished, however, they were all still out.

He went to the telephone. No dial tone.

"Shit," he hissed between clenched teeth. He flicked the receiver cradle up and down and checked the cord. Nothing. It was dead.

He looked around.

The motorcycles.

He grabbed a helmet and scanned the six parked bikes. The keys were in them. He chose an old black Yamaha 750 triple for its speed and pickup. He started to get on, when he noticed the red Norton. He had an idea.

He dismounted and went to side of the bike Seamus Killerbey had called the Red Devil. "Nobody rides her but me," he had told the other guards.

O'Toole grabbed a wrench. Working quickly, he removed the seat and took out one of the twelve-inch cylindrical bombards. He carefully removed the end where the firing pin was located. With a few quick strokes of a hacksaw the fuse was shortened to nothing. He put the bombard back together and delicately placed it back in its hiding place on the Norton.

The thing would go off with one good jolt. Seamus Killerbey wouldn't get halfway across the farmyard before he was blown to bits.

A few minutes later O'Toole was roaring up the narrow gravel road that led between the long stone walls enclosing the farm's fields. He stopped and scanned the rolling green countryside. The road led east and west. He didn't have the slightest clue which way to go.

"'Go west, young man,'" he muttered, and peeled away.

Ten minutes later he drove up to a small store and restaurant at a crossroads where the gravel met the paved highway. He was off the motorcycle and into the telephone booth outside the doors in a blur. He grabbed the receiver and started rattling the cradle. He dug into his pockets.

The operator came on.

He didn't have any money.

Who the fuck cared.

"Operator, it's an emergency. I want to call America. Collect."

THOUSANDS OF MILES WESTWARD, in his sixtieth-story office, Walker Jessup flipped through the collection of restaurant menus stacked in front of him on his desk. The leather-and-velveteen covers announced their provenance—they had been stolen from most of the better restaurants in New York City.

This was the Fixer's favorite time of day. This was when he perused the cuisines of his preferred dining spots, savoring the memory of dishes he'd tried, reminding himself of the culinary adventures that yet awaited.

From the far side of his office came the annoying clatter of the Telex machine. Interpol's latest. The most interesting scandal sheet in the world. Jessup moved quickly for a three-hundred-pounder. Down the room, past the long plate-glass window beyond which skyscrapers rubbed shoulders against a blue sky. He ripped the yellow sheet from the lips of the rollers and scanned it.

The usual.

A female member of parliament executed in Iran. A busful of schoolchildren turned into an incendiary bomb in Brazil. A grenade tossed into a hotel swimming pool by a Syrian terrorist in Greece. Armenians blowing up the theater at the French cultural center in Montreal. Still no news on the mysterious abduction of two American tourists from a hotel in Ireland.

Jessup yawned, dropped the Telex sheet in the circular file at his feet and returned to the menus on his desk. He had just settled in, when the phone rang. Sheeit. And the secretary was off.

"Hello. Walker Jessup."

A nasal voice, filled with static. "I have a collect call from Mr. Liam O'Toole in Armagh, Ireland, for a Mr. Walker Jessup. Will you accept the charges?"

Collect. Shit, Jessup thought. He'd just have to dock O'Toole's next paycheck.

IN THE NARROW PHONE BOOTH in Armagh County, Northern Ireland, O'Toole twisted and turned, keeping his eyes on the parking lot and road outside as the operator negotiated.

Please, please hurry, he prayed.

She came back on the line. "You may go ahead, sir."

"Walker! It's Liam."

"O'Toole, what do you—"

"I'm in trouble, Walker. Call Barrabas—" O'Toole saw something that silenced him momentarily: a man on a motorcycle had entered the parking lot. "Call Barrabas now! Get him to Susy's house. She needs—" The man dismounted and pulled a handgun from his jacket. He was walking toward the phone booth.

"Liam, what in hell's name is—"

"Jessup, she's in danger. I'm—"

O'Toole looked up. Into the big black eye of the gun and the twinkling eyes of Seamus Killerbey.

"I'm in—"

The gun blinked.

WALKER JESSUP HEARD AN EXPLOSION, followed by the clatter of a falling receiver. There was silence, then some muffled noises. Someone at the other end was listening.

"Hello?" Jessup said weakly. There was no answer. The receiver clicked as it was replaced in the cradle. The dial tone returned. Jessup put down the phone.

He sat for a moment, staring out the plate-glass window at the sky. He looked thoughtful. Then he looked disturbed. With considerable determination, he pushed his bulky frame up from his chair. He closed the menu that was open on top of the pile and placed the whole stack underneath the files on the Middle Eastern civil war he had arranged on instructions from the man who planned to be president when the carnage was over.

Jessup stood looking out the window again as the big brain put its twenty-odd years of intelligence expertise to work. He walked to the wastepaper can beside the Telex machine and pulled out the crumpled yellow newsprint. He stood there for several minutes, staring at the item about the missing tourists in Ireland.

6

The Wyoming sky was big and wide, the blueness bled out by feathery wisps of high-altitude clouds. Nile Barrabas closed the door of the ranch house behind him and stood on the wooden porch, surveying the land. It spread to the edge of the horizon.

In early spring the fields were still brown. The landscape was marred only by the long straight lines of barbed wire strung on posts, and a highway at the end of the dirt road that led up to his house. Several miles to the west was a smooth gash in the land, which marked the course of the Green River. The river was high now with spring runoff—he'd driven out yesterday to see it—but by June it would be little more than a murky creek at the bottom of a muddy chasm.

Barrabas knew this land better than anything in the world. Well, almost anything. He knew war better. This was the land he'd grown up on, the place he'd run away from when he was seventeen to join the Army.

The folks in the little town of Green River, twenty miles the other side of the horizon, considered him a hero because of all those Vietnam decorations the Pentagon had strung across his chest like lights on a Christmas tree.

"You coming back to settle down, Nile?" they'd ask in town every time he made one of his infrequent visits to the homestead. "That old place of yours needs someone to take care of it since your folks passed on."

With conspiratorial winks, the old geezers who sat on benches outside the main store and just down from the main bar and pool hall would tell him, "Got some mighty fine-looking ladies in these parts, Nile. You oughta settle down at the old place and find yourself a good-looking woman to take care of you."

Every time he'd laugh and answer, "I'm more trouble than I'm worth, fellas." He'd load his supplies into the back of the old pickup and head back out.

The old-timers would shake their heads and elbow one another like insiders on a roll. "That there Nile sure ain't no talkative fella, now is he?" one would lament.

"Nope," another would answer. "They say Vietnam made him like that. He didn't even show up to get the Medal of Honor from the President himself in Washington."

A third one would say, "Well, that there's one thing he won't abide no one talking about. Strikes me he quit the Army in a mighty huff. But all this traveling around the world, doing things he won't talk about—if you ask me it ain't good for a man to live like an island and think the rest of the world's agoin' to come lapping at his shore."

Then the three old men would nod sagely, righteous in their judgment, and wait to go through it all again the next time Nile came to town.

Nile Barrabas knew the kinds of things they said. The locals in these out-of-way places were always resentful when one of their own didn't partake of the community. That meant living, marrying and dying in the same place, and not much more. He'd been born in Green River. His grandfather was one of Wyoming's pioneers, the first man to till the soil and drive a herd of cattle across the Green River. For that reason alone, Nile Barrabas would always be welcome there.

In small places everyone is allowed to be a little strange in his own harmless way. The natives would talk about him when his back was turned, but ultimately they'd accept him, wishing the town prodigal son would come home to stay someday. Nile knew it would never happen.

He was taking a breather now. He was starting to accept the fact that his girlfriend, Erika Dykstra, had left him—looked like for good. For the time being he didn't have any other woman waiting in the wings—at least, none he really felt like calling up. So he had made his annual trip to the old family ranch.

It was quiet and peaceful, a far cry from the kind of places he worked in when Uncle Sam found him a secret dirty war to fight. And he spent the days in quiet meditation, thinking about nothing in particular as he put a few new shingles on the roof of the house and fixed the fences on the southern acreage.

The first item on this day's agenda was a drive into Green River to pick up the box of cigars he'd forgotten the day before. He smoked only a couple a day, but those times were moments he looked forward to, and he'd just run out of tobacco.

Before he got to the pickup truck, he saw a tawny station wagon barreling down the main highway in the distance. He watched it zip along and raise a cloud of dust as it turned without slowing into the dirt drive. The road was in bad shape from years of neglect. He had been meaning to get it fixed for years. Maybe he had never done so because he liked it that way. It discouraged visitors—usually. But today it looked as if someone were coming to him, potholes or not.

About half a mile away, the station wagon hit the worst of the potholes, bouncing down, then flying a foot into the air and crashing so hard he could hear the underside hit the dirt.

Maybe the visitor wouldn't make it. From the sounds of things, the muffler wouldn't.

The car came into the yard in front of the old house at full speed. The driver braked, but the car kept sliding, leaving deep furrows in the clay soil. It slid to halt with the bumper two feet from Barrabas's knees.

He recognized the driver.

Billy Two stepped out of the car.

Barrabas smiled broadly at the sight of the eccentric Indian. He'd been convinced Billy Two had gone peculiar after his experiences in the hands of the Russian military police and the doctors at that clinic outside Moscow. But Billy Two had proved since that he was still a helluva fighter.

In some ways, Barrabas liked the crazy guy best of all his hired soldiers. His smile faded when he saw the Osage's face.

Billy Two's normally dark skin was pale and his bloodshot eyes protruded from their sockets. The white shirt he wore was soiled with sweat and dirt. Billy stood there, all six foot two of him, and stared at Barrabas like a zombie. He looked as if he'd driven halfway across the continent on a nonstop burn.

"What's the matter, Billy?" Barrabas strode around the car to get closer. There was something strange about him. He realized then that the Indian wasn't blinking. His eyes stared glassily from their sockets, the lids frozen in place.

"Colonel, something's the matter." Billy Two saw the look of incomprehension that crossed Barrabas's face. He tried again. "Something's wrong. It's hard to explain, but . . . I know it. Someone is in big trouble. One of us."

Since the time Billy Two's mind had snapped at the hands of his torturers, Barrabas had gotten used to the Osage's wild inklings. He didn't have time for hocus-pocus himself, but he knew that on several occasions the wild man's instincts had been right on the money.

"Where've you come from, Billy?" he asked.

"Arizona."

"Without stopping?"

"For gas." Starfoot seemed ashamed to admit it.

"Let's go inside. First thing I'm going to do is make coffee. Then you can start at the beginning."

Barrabas started for the steps, with Billy following. Halfway across the porch he looked back at him.

"Billy, do me a favor?" Barrabas asked.

"Sure." Billy's facial expression remained frozen.

"Blink."

"What?"

"Your eyelids," he reminded him. "Blink."

It took a few seconds for Billy Two to understand. Then he blinked. Once. His eyelids went back up and stayed frozen in place.

Barrabas opened the front door, shaking his head. "Coffee first," he muttered.

IN HIS NEW YORK OFFICE, Walker Jessup looked at the telephone numbers scrawled on the scratch pad in front of him. A contact in the home secretary's office in Dublin had confirmed the worst. The two American tourists kidnapped from the Ashford Castle Hotel in County Mayo had been identified as Liam O'Toole and his wife, Susy Rourke. For some reason the lid was tight on information involving the case, and no details had been released to the media. The official didn't know why, but he knew where the pressure had come from: the American State Department.

"Why wasn't I informed?" the Fixer murmured.

The State Department would have run O'Toole's name through their computers and come up with a top-security designation, indicating special handling. Obviously they put out the orders to keep the media off. The last thing State wanted was for some hungry journalist to dig out the story of O'Toole's career as a professional soldier, of his association with Nile Barrabas and the rest of the SOBs. Since Walker Jessup was the sole contact between the House committee and

Barrabas's "dirty tricks" team, it would have been normal procedure for State to inform him.

The office intercom buzzed and his secretary's voice filtered through. An old friend of his in the State Department was returning his call.

Jessup explained the situation. "Why wasn't I informed?" he demanded.

The voice on the other end of the line sounded guarded. "Is this line secure?"

"Bloody right it is."

"First off, Walker, officially O'Toole has no status of any kind with the U.S. government or any of its security agencies. So it's impossible for him to be in any of our computers, even with a top-security designation."

Jessup nodded silently as the man spoke. He was right. Neither Barrabas nor any of the SOBs had any kind of status at all. They worked privately. For Jessup. The fact that they were instruments of American foreign policy, as determined by the secret House committee, was irrelevant. That way, if the boys ever fucked up, they were screwed, chewed and goosed.

The man from State continued. "Now between you and me, it appears that our government did receive notice from you that one Liam O'Toole had, uh, resigned his commission. Is that correct?"

Jessup coughed slightly. "Er, yes, but—"

"Well, shit, Walker. You know how these things work jurisdiction-wise. This guy's so sensitive that even his security designation is classified. There are people around here who like to know everything, and they get pissed off if they figure someone's got a party going that they're not invited to, if you know what I mean. As soon as certain people found out that this guy, who doesn't have any connection to the U.S. government in the first place, no longer has those nonconnections, know what I mean, then they figure that he's no longer in your jurisdiction, y'know. Anyway, since he's no longer your affair, and since he's officially never been anyone else's, well . . ."

"He got back-filed."

"He doesn't exist, Jessup. None of your, er, employees do. None of us knows anything about them. Know what I mean?"

"Thanks for the info, Michael."

"Anytime, Walker."

The Fixer hung up.

For a moment he stared at the view of Manhattan. Someone was going to be pissed off in a very big way. He shuddered to think about it. He picked up the phone and dialed Barrabas.

"WELL, YOU SEE, I get these feelings. I mean, like images in my head. And it's hard to describe the feeling that whatever it is is absolutely real. Or it's going to be real. I mean, I'm talking absolute conviction that these images are real. And then I hear voices. . . ."

Billy Two stopped talking for a moment. He could tell from the look in the Colonel's eyes that he was going to have a hard time getting this one through.

"So you say you're absolutely convinced that someone—one of the team—is in trouble. Or that they're going to be in trouble. But you don't know who." Barrabas got up and went to the stove, where he grabbed the pot of steaming hot coffee. He poured another cup for Billy Two and one for himself.

"I know it, Colonel. I really know it. I just wish I could explain it to you."

Barrabas nodded. In a way he did understand. But the story was too crazy to admit that.

"Well, then, let's—"

The telephone rang.

"Get on the phone," he finished as it rang again. "Although it sounds as if someone just beat us to it."

He left the room and picked up the receiver. Billy Two didn't listen to the conversation. Sitting in something that wasn't moving down a highway at close to a hundred miles an hour for the first time in two days made him feel light-headed. And every time he closed his eyes, he saw a long white line running by. At least he was blinking normally now.

Barrabas came back into the kitchen.

"Walker Jessup," the Colonel said in response to the unasked question.

Billy Two waited as the Colonel took his seat and looked across the table at him.

"Liam O'Toole. He's in big trouble."

IN ATLANTIC CITY, the party had risen to new heights of frenzy. The band played on wearily, out of time and out of tune, as half the members sat in their chairs, fast asleep, loosely clutching their instruments in their hands. Half a dozen well-dressed gate-crashers lay passed out in chairs and sofas throughout the penthouse suite.

The man in the tuxedo spent half the night screaming his lungs out in abject terror before settling into an endless pitiful whimper. When Beck hauled him up his mind was gone. He looked grateful and babbled incoherently. Nanos threw him out.

Meanwhile, management had begun their efforts to evict the two men from the hotel. First they cut off the flow of booze. It wasn't long before the freeloaders who had been lining up at the door began their departures to other scenes and other good times.

The two mercs spent the night joyfully, Nanos with the nips and Beck with the flanks. They ignored repeated phone calls from the desk, asking them if they were going to check out first thing in the morning.

When morning came, it brought the manager. He was a tall, heavy-set man with a scarred face and an expensive suit. He talked with a New York street accent, the kind guys pick up during their apprenticeships as pimps, or as enforcers in the protection business.

"Youse guys, I knows youse spent a lotta bucks here, but youse is causing me a lotta trouble, too. Like that guy youse hung outside the window. I'm going to have to ask youse to leave the hotel." He sounded almost apologetic.

Nanos listened to him with one hand on the door handle and the other holding his skimpy kung-fu robe together. Every time he blinked, his eyelids stuck. His mouth felt as if he'd been chewing toilet paper. Strange, he thought, considering where his mouth had been all night.

"Ya got it?" the manager said hoarsely. His tone was threatening. Nanos shut the door calmly in his face and bolted it.

Half an hour later, a helicopter was hovering outside the window. Inside it were two stern men wearing dark sunglasses. They weren't cops, and those weren't clarinets they held in their hands. They checked out all the windows in the two-story suite before disappearing into the wild blue yonder.

Then the action at the door started. It took them five minutes to bash the door down. Twenty cops streamed into the room like a convention at a Roach Motel. The manager was right behind them.

"Now I tries to be nice to youse guys, and what kind of tanx do I gets," he told Nanos and Beck sadly when the two struggling, naked men were brought to him by eight cops, one for each arm and leg. The other twelve officers were arguing over their assignments for helping the ladies out.

"I'll get you for this," Nanos screamed.

The manager appeared undisturbed. He turned to the plump policeman, who seemed to be in charge.

"Your boys can take care of these two," he said. "They needs a lesson."

"Sure, Mr. Ricotta. Anything you say." The plump policeman beamed in cold-blooded anticipation as Alex and Nate, naked, kicking and cursing, were dragged away.

7

Nanos and Beck were still naked when the police dropped them off at the end of a service road in the middle of a vast marsh near the New Jersey coast.

"If we get a complaint and have to haul you in for indecent exposure we'll throw the book at you," the plump sergeant threatened haughtily.

The two mercs cursed and yelled as they were thrown out, and Nanos even ran after the last departing police car, kicking the fender with his bare foot. He grabbed the foot and howled with pain.

"Nice day for a walk, boys, har-har!" The voice faded as Atlantic City's finest disappeared in clouds of gravel dust.

Far across the high brown grasses of endless marshland was an elevated freeway. Even farther in the distance, industrial plants smoked busily away in the low, white sky.

The two men surveyed their surroundings. It was getting cold.

"Beautiful New Jersey." Nanos said it without enthusiasm.

"Yeah. My mother always warned me about New Jersey."

"But you grew up in New York!"

"Yeah," Nate said, nodding. "That's why."

The two men stood silently a moment, until Nate asked the sixty-four-million-dollar question.

"What do we do now?"

Nanos looked at him, surprised. "We walk."

Beck looked thoughtful.

"What's on your mind?"

"Those flanks."

Both men laughed. Then they walked.

WALKER JESSOP TURNED THE CAR onto the wide suburban street and cruised gracefully past the ranch-style houses in his green BMW. Two kids ran into the street, chasing a baseball. The Fixer aimed for them. The kids looked up, terrified at the sudden onslaught of the expensive German import. They forgot about the ball and hightailed it back into the yard they had unluckily emerged from.

"Don't like kids, Jessup?" Nile Barrabas inquired from the passenger's seat.

"Nope." The big Texan shot straight from the hip.

In the back seat, Billy Starfoot had turned white— an accomplishment, considering the normal color of his burnished brown skin.

They had arrived in New York by lunchtime— barely an hour ago. Jessup had met them at the airport. Immediately they had decided to drive out to Susy Rourke's home in outlying Newark. Barrabas didn't know what he'd find there—certainly not Liam O'Toole or his wife, since no one was answering the phone. But a gut instinct told him to go. Besides, they had four hours to kill before the next flight to Dublin.

On the Colonel's instructions, Jessup had been on the phone all morning, trying to round up the rest of the SOBs. Lee Hatton and Geoff Bishop had disappeared to Bishop's lodge on a northern lake in the forests of Canada. Bishop had a small private airplane to take them down to Montreal, where they would connect with a flight from Mirabel, meeting the others in Belfast that evening. But Alex Nanos and Nate Beck had completely disappeared.

Several phone calls to their hotel in Atlantic City had elicited the curt response that the two mercs had "checked out." It was against the rules not to leave a forwarding address for Jessup, just as it was necessary for Barrabas to be available at all times. None of them voiced the question nagging all three of them: were Nate Beck and the Greek messed up in Liam O'Toole's disappearance?

"This is it," Jessup said, slowing a little as they passed a long white bungalow with cute green shutters. "Three fifty-seven." He drove past it half a block to an intersection and parked near a school yard and some other cars. As anonymous as they appear to an outsider, the suburbs are one of the hardest places in the world for an outsider to appear inconspicuous. Everyone watches.

"Need some help?" Jessup turned to Barrabas when the car was parked.

"Billy Two," Barrabas said to the Indian in the back seat. "Walker, you wait here and keep an eye on things. I don't know why I'm here, but it's always possible we'll be leaving in a hurry.''

The two mercs approached the house and rang the doorbell. The curtains were drawn across the windows, and the bell echoed as though it were ringing in an empty house. Curtains moved in the window of the house across the street.

''Slip around back, Billy. See if there's anything interesting. I'll stay here in case the neighbors are watching.''

Billy Two melted away behind the low row of cedar trees that ran up against the house. Barrabas rang again. He waited a minute for Billy Two to return, and rang one last time. He heard footsteps from inside, and the sound of the locks being turned. The door was opened a crack and then swung wide.

''Come on in.'' Billy Two smiled and unlocked the screen door. Barrabas moved smoothly inside.

''The locks on these houses are designed to keep only the honest people out,'' he told the Colonel.

''No one home?''

''Not as far as I can see.''

The two men fanned into the house, explored the rooms and met back in the hall.

''Nothing?''

Billy Two shook his head.

''I'm going to look around a bit more.''

Barrabas went slowly through the house, opening closets and drawers, not really knowing what he was looking for. In a bedroom drawer he found an old color photograph of Liam's wife as a young girl, standing beside a handsome man with a saucy smile.

"That her?" Billy Two asked, coming into the room and looking over Barrabas's shoulder.

"Yeah, I think so. When she was a teenager, I guess."

Something about the photograph bothered Barrabas. He couldn't put his finger on it. The man looked familiar.

"You know her well?" Starfoot asked.

Barrabas shook his head. "Only met her once." He slipped the photograph inside his jacket. "Let's get out of here."

As they left the house by the front door, the curtains across the street wavered slightly once again.

"Shit," Barrabas cursed under his breath as the two men walked to the street. Both men avoided looking at the house.

"They do it on purpose, you know, Colonel. Spy on their neighbors, intentionally making it obvious so their neighbors *know* they're being watched."

"I hope that's it." They headed toward the green BMW, half a block away.

"Sure it is. It's human nature. In Russia they institutionalize it. Here, with good old American know-how, we do it socially. For free."

As they climbed into the car, Jessup looked up curiously. Barrabas shook his head. The men rode in grim silence as Jessup steered his car through the maze of identical streets back to the freeway.

"What's the exact time we rendezvous with Hatton and Bishop in Belfast?" Barrabas asked Jessup finally.

"You arrive at 2200 hours in Dublin, make your connection and land in Belfast an hour later. Hatton and Bishop will already be there."

"That would be 4:00 A.M. Irish time, Barrabas figured, thinking out the next step. He had an old British army buddy who was stationed in Belfast who might help. And Lee Hatton would probably have some intelligence contacts left over from her days as an undercover agent for some of Washington's secret agencies.

"Colonel," Billy Two said from the back seat, "what do you see way over there?" He pointed out the car window. They were traveling on a freeway that led straight across a broad flat marshland near the Atlantic coast.

Barrabas squinted and looked at two figures walking toward the highway on a service road.

"Looks like a couple of nudists who wandered away from camp."

"Where?" said Jessup, glancing around. It was the best thing he'd heard all day.

"Colonel..." Billy Two began. He had a reputation for having the best eyesight of all the SOBs. Consequently he was the best sharpshooter.

"I don't believe it," Barrabas said, recognizing the two naked men. "Yeah...yeah, I believe it," he said, changing his mind. "Walker, you better pull off onto the service road at the exit up ahead there."

"What is it? Who is it?" Jessup shrieked impatiently, gawking around and trying to drive at the same time.

"Don't ask," Barrabas told him.

Billy Two burst into peals of laughter. He rolled down the window and let out one of his bloodcurdling war whoops. There was no mistaking the Osage warrior's distinctive battle cry. Even at a distance of almost half a kilometer, Nanos and Beck recognized it. The two looked up and saw Jessup's green BMW bearing down on them. They ran to meet it. The back door swung open, and Billy Two's grinning face welcomed them inside.

"Gee, I've never been happier to see you in my life," Nanos said, climbing in with a faceful of teeth. It was a good try, but the look of relief in his eyes was obvious. "How'd you guys know we were here?"

Nate Beck slammed the door closed and huddled in a chilling, embarrassed silence. "Fuckers," he cursed once, his voice low and angry.

"We didn't," Billy Two said. "We were just out for a drive." His eyes met Barrabas's as the Colonel looked at the two nude refugees in the back seat.

"It was those bastards at the hotel," Nanos spluttered. "They're paying off the fucking police—"

"Can it," Barrabas ordered. "I don't even want to know." He took off his coat and handed it back. "Cover it up. It ain't pretty."

Billy Two handed over his jacket, as well. Jessup gave the two men a long sorry look over his shoulder and pulled back onto the freeway.

"Where're you going?" Nanos asked weakly. Nate Beck was still simmering in silence.

Jessup told them the story. Nanos fell as silent as Beck. The car approached the Lincoln Tunnel which would take them into Manhattan. Both mercs felt a deep sense of shame. It wasn't unusual to go wild between missions, packing all the living you could into what little time you had. All Barrabas's soldiers were intense, each in his own way. But this time around, Nanos and Beck had overshot the margin. They had fucked up: at a crucial moment they hadn't been available. This job was an important one. O'Toole had been Barrabas's second in command, the guy who made the rest of the mercs toe the line. He was a good buddy, as well.

"I'm glad you guys showed up," Nanos said finally. He had lost the blustering bravado of a few minutes earlier. "If Liam's in trouble, I want to be there to help take care of it."

"What about the others?" Nate Beck spoke at last. "Who else is coming?"

"Hatton and Bishop are in Canada. They're leaving for Ireland about now and should meet us in Belfast tonight," Starfoot told them.

"Right. The two lovebirds. Bishop's going to get his—"

Billy Two elbowed the Greek. "You never stop, do you, Alex?"

Nanos lapsed into a sulky silence.

"And Hayes?" Beck asked.

Billy shrugged. From the front seat Jessup answered. "Claud's busy. He took another job for me. In Africa. With the Colonel's permission. Right now I couldn't get hold of him if I tried."

The car was sailing through the streets of New York now. Jessup steered sideways through the heavy traffic until he could pull over to the curb. Pedestrians and cabdrivers alike did a double take when they saw the two seminaked men.

"Can you arrange for passports in time?" Barrabas asked Jessup.

The big Texan wordlessly opened the compartment between the two front seats and took out the car phone. "It'll cost, but my favorite forger can do rush jobs." He dialed.

Barrabas got out and closed the car door.

"Where are we?" Nanos asked, uncomfortably aware of the stares of passersby.

Jessup put his hand over the mouthpiece. "Bloomingdale's. You boys need some clothes. The plane to Dublin leaves in less than two hours."

8

The next morning, Nile Barrabas walked down Garmoyle Street in Belfast. The steady morning drizzle was already getting tiresome. The street bordered one side of the Victoria Channel, an arm of water from the Belfast Lough, the harbor, that cut into the center of the city.

He had arrived with Starfoot, Nanos and Beck less than twelve hours earlier on a shuttle flight from Dublin and had been swept up in a whirl of security procedures. Their hand luggage had been taken from them at Shannon and sealed in plastic bags before the plane departed. In Belfast, the airport was filled with gangly, young British soldiers, dressed in ill-fitting leisure suits and loud plaids, returning from leave.

Hatton and Bishop were waiting for them. The mercs decided to split up and book into separate hotels to avoid being conspicuous. The hotels would undoubtedly have spies who channeled information to the various warring underground armies of the city.

The last the Colonel saw of Nanos, Beck and Billy Two, they were phoning small hotels, trying to make reservations. For some reason, whenever Nanos or

Beck gave their names, the desk clerks quickly remembered they didn't have more rooms, after all.

"We've been blacklisted," Nate Beck said as the horror dawned on him.

"What did you guys do in Atlantic City?" Starfoot asked incredulously.

The Greek went wide-eyed and innocent. "Nothing, Billy, just a party. Like the ones we used to have. Remember?"

Billy Two did. He winced.

"I don't even want to know," the Colonel commented, leaving them to fend for themselves.

The sky rumbled threateningly over distant rooftops, and the drizzle turned into a rain that pounded down in large hard drops. Barrabas turned in at the Great Boar, a typical Irish pub near the car-ferry terminal. He casually took in the iron-plated front doors and the screen of thick steel cables that covered the big plate-glass windows. It was like walking into a cage. Lee Hatton and Geoff Bishop were waiting for him at the bar. A few other clients were scattered in booths along the dark walls. A coal fire, burning in an ornate old cast-iron fireplace, threw a searing heat into the center of the room.

Lee Hatton was a tall, slim woman with short dark hair. The well-developed muscles of the professional soldier were disguised by the svelte lines of her clothing. Hatton was the team's medical expert, and when they were in the field she fought like an angry tigress.

She had been one of the original SOBs. Bishop had come aboard later, when Al Chen bought it in the Iranian desert and Barrabas needed an expert pilot on the team. Bishop had learned the ropes as a decorated pilot in the Canadian Air Force. He had gotten his experience in antiterrorist warfare from his postings in Crete and the Gaza.

"Welcome to Belfast," Barrabas said quietly to the mercs. The bartender threw him a demanding look. He glanced at what Lee and Geoff were drinking. "Guinness," he said curtly.

"It'd be good to see you, Colonel, if it weren't for the circumstances," Bishop told him.

"Anything more to go on than what you told us yesterday?" Lee asked.

Barrabas shook his head and waited while the bartender brought over a quart-sized glass of brown stout with a three-inch-thick head spilling off the top. It dripped over the bar as he set the glass down.

"Nothing. I'm going to see an old friend who's a major in the British Army here. I was posted with him in Germany once a long time ago. I'll see what he has to say."

"What about transportation? I guess you don't know about air power yet."

"Helicopters usually come in handy. Look around and see what's available. For ground transportation, too. I do know we'll need guns. I want you to find us some, Lee."

She laughed and nodded, her brown eyes sparkling mischievously. This was the attitude that had put her through most of the secret agencies in Washington. She was the daughter of a famous U.S. Army general, and she had lived around power all her life. It didn't faze her one bit—and that made her a powerful woman in her own right.

"I guess I can track down a few people," she said, her eyes looking up as she clicked through a mental file. "There's a big enough underground market here. Shouldn't be a problem."

"Have you seen—"

Just as Barrabas started to ask, Alex Nanos, Billy Starfoot and Nate Beck came into the Great Boar, the doors slamming behind them with a heavy metal crash.

The Greek pushed his thick wet hair back out of his face and brushed the raindrops off his coat. All three were soaking wet.

"I am too loyal for my own good," Billy Two said darkly as he came to the bar. The downpour had plastered the Indian's long black hair down his cheeks and neck.

Nanos's eyes lit up when he saw the fireplace. He went straight to it. "Heat," he moaned thankfully, closing his eyes and stretching out his hands to toast them.

Beck stripped his soaking coat off and greeted Hatton and Bishop.

"I guess you guys found a place to stay last night," Barrabas said slowly.

Nate rubbed his neck as he nodded.

Billy Two's eyebrows lowered an inch. "What claims to be a bed and breakfast down near the docks. It was on the fifth floor, in rooms built for dwarfs. There were bedbugs in the straw mattresses, and the things growing on the walls could defeat Russia in biological warfare.''

Nate nodded sadly. "And around four in the morning we were awakened by a herd of cattle, mooing and bellowing in terror as they were driven into a slaughterhouse.''

Nanos joined them. "Yeah, it was the only place we could get. They were booked up everywhere else. You guys were lucky. You got the last rooms in the city. Hi, Lee.'' Alex gave the doctor a happy smile. The Greek wasn't fazed by hardship. "What's on, Colonel?'' He rubbed the palms of his hands rapidly together for friction heat and blew a mouthful of hot air on his fingers.

"You make it look more like we're in Siberia in winter than Belfast in the spring,'' Bishop commented lightly.

"Yeah, well. If not Siberia, Canada.'' Nanos said thickly, without looking at the Canadian. "What's on, Colonel?'' he repeated.

"Nothing until we get some information. Beck—'' Barrabas turned to the team's computer expert.

The short stocky New York native had proved his eligibility for the team by arranging a computer-fraud scheme that skimmed the nickels and dimes off hundreds of thousands of bank accounts, until they added up to a million dollars. Barrabas had been fortunate to get to him minutes before Interpol showed up with an arrest warrant.

In the computer age anything is possible. When Nate started working for Barrabas, he didn't have the same fighting skills as the others, who had all come from military backgrounds. But the work was a dream come true for a brilliant but lonely electronics wizard with a big house, a big car and a wife who didn't understand him. He made a choice he never regretted when he decided he'd never see Beverley again. Instead of being a family man, he turned himself into a fighter, and his computer expertise was invaluable for the covert-action team that Barrabas led.

Men ruled the world, but information was power. And since most of it was now stored on computers, all Nate Beck had to do was push a few plastic buttons.

"O'Toole phoned Jessup from somewhere in Northern Ireland," Barrabas told Beck. "An operator handled the call because it was collect. Is there any way you can figure out where he dialed from?"

Nate thought a moment and nodded slowly. "If I tap into the phone company's records, sure. Simple. Take a few hours." He looked momentarily puzzled and turned to Starfoot. "Does our hotel have electricity?"

"It might even have running water," returned Billy Two.

"Dr. Hatton has her instructions," Barrabas continued. "Bishop, we need some ground transportation. A jeep or a Land Rover. Something with a bit of speed that will go anywhere."

"I'll take care of it, Colonel," the pilot promised.

Barrabas looked at his watch. "It's ten-thirty. Alex and Billy, I want you to stay put in case I need some backup. If the phone over there rings—" he pointed to the tiny wooden cubicle near the door "—it might be me. We'll all meet back here late this afternoon. At five.''

Barrabas was the first to leave the pub. The heavy rain and the drizzle had stopped, but the clouds were so low a tall man could reach up and touch them. The streets were filling with people. Barrabas checked the map in his breast pocket and headed east, past the docks and warehouses that lined the channel, to Newtownards Road and a small Catholic enclave called ''the Strand.'' He had one other person to see before visiting his friend the Major at British Army Headquarters.

This was the neighborhood Liam O'Toole had grown up in, and it probably hadn't changed much since he had left and gone to America. The crumbling brick houses were grimy, and the sidewalks and streets a lattice of potholes, cracks and missing paving stones. The few stores and pubs were barricaded by walls of sandbags in front of their windows.

Surrounded by Belfast Lough and the great shipyards on two sides and Protestant neighborhoods on the other two, the Strand was a besieged enclave. It was little wonder that this area produced the IRA's toughest, most ruthless fighters.

Barrabas found the little house. It looked the same as all the others on the narrow street. The steps sagged and shingles hung precariously from the eaves, but the curtains in the window were white and neatly hung, and the old brass handle on the front door had been recently polished.

The person who lived here, like most other poor people, did the best she could with what she had. It had always haunted Liam O'Toole that he couldn't do anything about it. This was the house he had grown up in, and his mother still lived here. O'Toole had made some tragic blunders as a teenager, long enough ago that it didn't matter anymore. But O'Toole's widowed mother hadn't forgotten. Or, as far as Barrabas knew, forgiven.

O'Toole was a tough guy, but the wound from the past festered in him. It was his one area of vulnerability, and Barrabas knew, because he had shared more than one long drinking bout with him. When the Irish-American was three sheets to the wind, he'd break into long recitations of the strange poetry he wrote in his head and then burst into tears for what had happened so long ago.

Barrabas knocked lightly on the door and waited. He soon heard the rustling of footsteps in the hallway, then a hand on the inside bolts. The door opened on a tiny, white-haired woman. Her hands, gnarled by too many years of hard work, clutched the door, and she stared suspiciously at the tall, muscular American with the white crew cut.

"I don't think I want any," she said, surveying him. For a second her sharp green eyes glinted with amusement.

"My name is Nile Barrabas. Can I talk with you? It's important. It's about your son."

"And what does an American want to talk to me about my sons for? And which son, since I've three of them? Padraic, Roy or Devan?" Her accent rolled off her tongue like foam riding the waves of the Irish Sea. "Or maybe you're another of those meddling Americans come to recruit the boys for the Provos." She looked at him with obvious defiance.

"No, ma'am. You've got another son. It's about him. Liam."

A look of surprise crossed the old woman's face, followed by a grimace of pain. Her lips tightened, and she tried to push the door closed without another word.

Barrabas wedged his foot in the door.

"It's very important. It could mean life or death. For Liam. For your son."

"I know not that man. I have but three sons, and none is named Liam." She said this angrily, turning and walking back into the house. Barrabas closed the door behind him and followed her inside.

She stood in the kitchen near an old-fashioned washboard, looking through a window to the small garden behind the house.

"Liam's a friend of mine. He came back to Ireland with his new wife, and they were abducted, probably by the IRA Provos. He's in trouble. I—and some other friends of his—came to find him. We need help. I need to know…anything that might lead us to him."

"The Devil takes his own kind," Mrs. O'Toole said sharply, refusing to turn and face Barrabas. For a moment there was a silence between them.

"Liam O'Toole's not IRA, ma'am. He's a fighter because some men have that calling in life. But he's a good man, and when all his deeds are put in the balance, it will be the Devil's loss."

"I've told you once, Mr. Barrabas. I have no son named Liam O'Toole."

From upstairs a woman's voice called out. "Mother, who is it?"

Mrs. O'Toole turned around finally. She looked frightened, torn. She could deny her son as long as she lied to Barrabas, but he clearly brought back painful memories, and they showed in her flecked green eyes. There were footsteps on the stairs.

"It's no one, dear. A man came looking for someone. He's made a mistake." Suddenly she put her hand to her throat and burst into a fit of coughing.

A young woman with short blond hair came into the kitchen. Barrabas turned around to look at her. The woman could have been beautiful, but one side of her face was shriveled with ghastly scar tissue.

"My daughter, Ellen Lorraine." Mrs. O'Toole said. "This is Mr. Barrabas from America. He is looking for someone, but he's made a mistake."

Barrabas nodded toward Liam's sister. "I'm sorry to bother you," he said, moving toward the front door. Mrs. O'Toole started coughing again uncontrollably, until her daughter put her arm around her. She turned away from Barrabas.

The Colonel paused at the front door and looked back. Mrs. O'Toole had stopped coughing now. Ellen Lorraine looked at him anxiously. He met her eyes and made his last comment.

"Mrs. O'Toole, you may say what you like about the Devil, but it's him that never forgives and never forgets."

He reached for the door handle to let himself out. In the kitchen, Ellen Lorraine let go of her aged mother. "I'll show him out," she said, walking quickly into the front hall. She came to the door just as Barrabas stepped outside.

"You're looking for Liam," she said, searching his face.

Barrabas stopped. "Liam was in Ireland, but he disappeared. I'm trying to find him."

"He's not been here, but I don't need to tell you that. Our mother—she...she won't abide even the mention of his name. She's..." The young woman's voice lowered and became sad. "She has cancer, you know. She won't be with us much longer."

"I'm sorry. Look, is there anything you can think of that might help me find Liam? Like, for instance, who might be after him and why?"

Ellen Lorraine shook her head sadly. "No... nothing. It's been years since I've seen—" She stopped midsentence, and glanced up at Barrabas. "Something just came to mind. It was something said at a church social a few years ago. Some of the neighborhood boys got all snapped up on whiskey and one of them told me something terrible about Liam. A terrible story."

"What was that?"

"Well, it's hardly believable, really. And after the lad said it, his friends told him off and apologized. It was about a local hero, a man named Tom Murphy, who was the leader of the IRA when Liam was..." Her voice faded as she felt the shame of Liam's indiscretion.

"Go on. I heard about Tom Murphy. He was shot by the British when they cornered him at a country farmhouse."

"Well, the boy said it was Liam's fault. He said if my brother ever set foot in Ireland again he'd face the music. If you find anything out, can you let me know? The rest of us, we don't feel the same way anymore. I only wish...before she..."

"I will. I promise," Barrabas told her. "If you hear anything else, I'm at the Donegal Hotel."

He turned and walked back to the street. A drizzle had started up again. He pulled up his collar and started walking.

A HUNDRED KILOMETERS AWAY, at the old farm in Armagh, Seamus Killerbey was staring at the milk truck with the nine mortars hidden in the van, his face dark with anger. The three guards stood silently on the sidelines, chastened and bruised from the beating they'd received from Liam O'Toole the day before.

"I want to hear it again," Killerbey growled. "Exactly as it happened."

The three men looked at one another uncomfortably. Rion spoke up. "He was working on the remote. He told us he had it fixed up and was going to show us. Then..."

Killerbey picked up the metal remote box from the back of the van and ripped off the metal cover. He sat down and examined the inside carefully, taking it apart piece by piece with a screwdriver.

"Right. Now I see what the bastard was up to," he said shortly. "He's fixed it so it'll short and send out the wrong signal. Bloody bastard. That'll fix it." He set the box down. "I warned you, didn't I, 'e'd be a tricky fellow?'' He stretched his arms out and yawned comfortably.

"Rion, you'll drive the milk wagon. Danny and I'll follow on the motorcycles."

"Today?" Danny said, surprised.

"We've no more time to waste on the matter, lad!" Killerbey said with annoyance. "Besides, I've the perfect place in mind, and by the time we're there, they'll just be sitting down to lunch."

Danny headed for one of the bikes and began to strap on the helmet. "You taking the Red Devil this time, Seamus?"

The IRA looked at the Norton, with the bombards hidden under the tank. He shook his head. "Not this time, lads. I'll have need of it later. Let's get moving!"

"What's the target?" Rion asked.

Killerbey's eyes sparkled. "British military intelligence headquarters, just off Newtownards Road." He was smiling with anticipation.

9

The British army headquarters was only a few blocks away from the impoverished Catholic neighborhood where Mrs. O'Toole lived. Barrabas waited at the gates of the compound while a serious guard scrutinized him, comparing what he saw against the picture in the passport. He spoke several words into a phone and finally smiled.

"Major Topman will see you now, Colonel. Er, we'll have to search you, if you don't mind," he said apologetically.

A few moments later, a young adjutant led the American on a brisk walk across the compound yard into the brick Victorian building. It looked as though it had once been an old school. Their shoes clicked on the hard shiny floors as they passed through long, high-ceilinged hallways. Finally the adjutant stopped and opened a frosted-glass office door.

Barrabas walked through into a large open room crowded with desks, telephones and files and continued past the personnel busy carrying out the elaborate paperwork that came with any army command. A group of five young privates waited nervously at a table behind the glass wall of a conference room. Major Topman came out of his office and walked toward Barrabas with a big welcoming smile.

The two soldiers shook hands and looked each other over.

"Saigon, wasn't it?" the British commander said.

Barrabas nodded. "Just before the fall."

Topman laughed. "I was smart. I got out before the big rush."

"And I was the last man."

"That's right. That was a great photograph of you grabbing on to the helicopter sled just as it left the top of the U.S. Embassy."

"Yeah. The journalist missed the Vietcong bullet that grazed my knuckles."

"Come on into my office. We can have a bit of privacy," Major Topman told him. As they crossed the room, Major Topman stuck his head into the conference room where the five young soldiers waited. They jumped fearfully to attention, shoulders back and chins up.

"At ease, men!" Topman told them. "You're the volunteers this week, is that right?"

"That's right, sir!" all five shouted in unison.

"None of you is married?"

"No, sir!"

Major Topman walked into the room and did a curt inspection of the rank. "Now we all realize that the job for which you have volunteered is not in the line of the usual services provided by Her Majesty's army."

"Yes, sir!"

"Nevertheless, in wartime, every soldier must be prepared to do whatever is necessary for the good of the kingdom."

"Yes, sir!"

"You soldiers are to be commended for responding to a request for volunteers to do a job above and beyond the call."

"Sir!"

Major Topman's tone took on a paternal quality. "And I trust that due to the nature of this job, you all realize that a great deal of discretion must be shown. In other words, soldiers, keep it under your hat. She's a voracious wench, but I understand—" Topman winked "—she can show a young soldier a capital time."

The young men laughed nervously just as a red-haired Scottish sergeant came into the room.

"Right, men!"

Fear showed in the faces of the soldiers as they snapped to attention.

"Major!" The sergeant saluted. "The volunteer party is ready and able, sir!"

"Right, sergeant. Fifteen Twaddell Avenue. Her name is Nula McGillivry and she'll be waiting. Remember, men!" Topman roared. "Her Majesty's reputation is in your hands."

The soldiers filed out of the room.

"All our reputations are in your hands, actually...." Topman muttered to himself.

He took Barrabas's elbow and steered him to his office, closing the door behind them. His desk was thick with papers, manuals and reports, piled as high as the top of the little flagpole that held a gauze Union Jack. Behind him, next to a picture of the queen, was a large map of Ireland, speckled with colored pins marking various military operations. One wall was mainly taken up by a large clear-glass window that looked out on the filing clerks and secretaries busy at their desks.

"What was that all about?" Barrabas asked.

"One of our more unusual operations," Topman said. "That's what I'm in charge of here. Military intelligence. Bloody good at it, too, if I do say so myself. The word from London is that in another year I can pick and choose my next posting."

"And that one?" Barrabas jerked his head toward the office on the other side of the glass partition.

Topman winked and raised his eyebrows. "One of our best informers is this Miss Nula McGillivry, a single woman who lives out past Falls Road. Her information is almost always accurate. Don't know how she gets it, really. But her price is unusual."

"I think I get the general idea."

"Exactly. Once a week I send out five young volunteers full of juice, to satisfy her rather large appetite. In exchange, she tell tales. It's a convenient arrangement. I never lack for volunteers, and I manage to keep morale up, as well. The best damn source of information I have. Clever, what? And what brings you to Ireland, Nile?"

Barrabas laughed. "You're still up to those kind of tricks. I remember the mah-jongg gambling parlors you funded through the British embassy in the Chinese quarter of Saigon."

"My waitresses serviced the gamblers and squeezed more information out of them than all the rest of my legitimate agents put together." Topman chortled with the memory. He stopped abruptly and looked at Barrabas, ready to get down to business.

"A friend of mine disappeared. He was abducted from a hotel in the Republic a few days ago."

"Hmm, that would be..." Topman rolled his eyes upward. "O'Toole, wasn't it. Someone O'Toole. And his wife, too, if I recall."

"Liam O'Toole. So you know about it."

"Of course I know about it—I mean, that it happened. Came in the day's round of police bulletins. But other than that I don't know anything, and I don't know this O'Toole or his wife. You have to understand, Nile, kidnappings and executions and bombings are a dime a dozen in this land. The streets are wet with blood here."

"So what's being done about it?"

"Here? Nothing whatsoever. In Southern Ireland, the police will put out their reports and do some routine investigation, but if the IRA was involved in this, the police won't turn up much." With the fingers of one hand, Topman played with some papers on the corner of his desk. "Would the IRA have been involved in this, Nile?" he asked casually.

Barrabas waited a moment before answering. "Probably."

"And why would that be?"

"O'Toole had some involvement with them years ago. I don't know the details. But he left and emigrated to America. He was my 2IC in Vietnam.

Whatever the case back then, I know he's renounced the IRA since. In fact, since he got married, he's given up soldiering completely.''

"Perhaps that's why the IRA were interested in him. They don't like people who renounce them. Once you're in, there's no way out."

At that moment the frosted glass of the office door rattled under a firm knock. A group of army officers and military police stood with a civilian, an odd-looking man with dull eyes and a simple expression. He wore plaid knit pants and a jacket that didn't match, and he looked about the room, wide-eyed with wonder.

"Come in!" Major Topman bellowed.

A prim officer with an efficient look about him stepped inside and saluted.

"At ease, Captain Keenly." Major Topman returned a careless salute. "What have you got?"

The officer's eyes wavered in Barrabas's direction.

"Oh, by the way," Topman boomed, "let me introduce you to an old buddy of mine. Colonel Nile Barrabas, U.S. Army."

"Retired," Barrabas added, standing and shaking hands with the captain.

"You can speak up. Colonel Barrabas used to be in this line of work himself. Probably still is, though he wouldn't tell me if he was, isn't that right, Colonel?" Topman gave Barrabas a curious look.

"Sir, this is the chap I spoke to you about for the operation. His name is McVaghey and he's a bit daft, but I think he'll do."

"I have every confidence in you, Captain Keenly." Topman opened his top desk drawer and withdrew a package of cigarettes. They were British-made, and the box was the cardboard kind with a sliding drawer. He pushed it open. Inside, standing in the row of filter cigarettes, were several bullets. "Here they are. I trust the RUC have been informed what to look for and where to look."

"Of course, sir."

"Then let's get moving on it. I want to flush these bastards out once and for all." He held up the cigarette packet for Barrabas to see. "This man has agreed to do a little work for us. He'll let us plant this ammo in his house exactly where the local police will be sure to find it. In return, Mr. McVaghey will be notified of the time of the raid on his home, and thus will be able to avoid being arrested."

"Some deal," Barrabas said, a little surprised. "He lets you set him up and in exchange you get him off."

"Ah, yes." Major Topman smiled secretively. "But he'll immediately turn to a certain parish priest for help. We suspect this priest of being the open end of the conduit that leads into the IRA escape routes and underground." Topman leaned forward and lowered his voice. "It's true the man is simple," he said confidentally. "But I've always believed the secret to this kind of work is to use people's natural talents."

"Sir!" Keenly took the doctored cigarette package. "I was wondering, sir, if I could go over certain details of the operation, sir."

"Er, ah . . ." Major Topman looked surprised, but it was obvious that Captain Keenly wanted to discuss it in private. "Yes, quite so," he said reluctantly. "Er..."

"Let me make a phone call. I'll be back in a few minutes."

"Fine, Nile. We'll need only a minute."

Barrabas walked past the line of MPs and the two officers of the Royal Ulster Constabulary in police blue who stood around Simon McVaghey. A look in the man's dull, unhappy eyes told Barrabas instantly that the poor fellow didn't know what was going on. He was both flattered and frightened by all the attention he was getting—the classic personality profile of someone who habitually fucks up.

Barrabas found a row of pay phones at the end of the hallway. He dialed the number of the Great Boar. The phone rang twice and was yanked off the cradle.

"Hello!" Nanos. The voice was firm and willful. The Greek had it together again.

"Take a name and an address."

"Got it, Colonel." Alex fumbled inside his jacket in the cramped little phone box at the public house. He figured it was built for leprechauns.

"Her name is Nula McGillivry, and she lives at 15 Twaddell Avenue."

Nanos whistled. "Lovely name."

"It seems appropriate," Barrabas said. "She supplies military intelligence with some of their best information, and as a reward they send over five of their itchiest to service her."

"For queen and country, Colonel.... You want Billy and me to stake her out?"

"Yeah, starting now. Uh . . . I figure it's up your alley, Alex."

Nanos looked at the telephone receiver in his hand. He couldn't believe the Colonel was putting him up to this. Nula McGillivry! The name conjured up a vision of red-haired, green-eyed beauty.

"Got it, Colonel."

Barrabas hung up.

"Hey, Billy!" Nanos shouted as he scrambled from the phone booth. "You're not going to believe this!"

Barrabas returned to Major Topman's office. Keenly, McVaghey and the retinue of police were gone. The British officer was blowing the dust off the base of the little Union Jack on his desk.

"So you can see I'm quite busy here," he said as Barrabas came back in. "Lots of irons in the little fire called Northern Ireland. And how those IRA bastards would like to get me, too. I'm at the top of their death list right now."

"What kind of help can you give me with O'Toole?"

"Not a bloody great deal, Nile, I'm sorry to say." He settled back in his swivel chair and folded his hands in his lap. His voice was suddenly cool. "Not much to go on, is there? Tell you what, Nile. I'll have one of my officers, a good one, too, look into it and give me a report. The police in the Republic of Eire are called the Garda. I'll have him check their reports on this abduction, and whatever else is around. But frankly, Nile, we don't usually make much progress on these things unless something comes to us. And usually it's a body."

"What about Tom Murphy, the IRA leader who was killed a few years ago by your men?"

"Shot while trying to escape, as I recall. What about him?"

"How did you people know how to find his hideout?"

Major Topman pursed his lips and thought a moment. "We had an informer on that one, as I recall. It was before my time, but I've read the history. Let me see. I think I still have a file here."

He swiveled in his desk chair to the filing cabinet behind him and took out a thin red file. "Yes. It was after a bomb went off inside the munitions supply depot at British army headquarters. One of the fellows arrested in the subsequent roundup talked."

He flipped the file closed and looked up at Barrabas.

"Who?" Barrabas's question was to the point.

"Well, really, old chap. That's highly classified information. I could lose my job over that. You really ought not to ask."

Barrabas nodded slowly. "Then I'll keep looking around myself."

Major Topman suddenly looked a little agitated. "What exactly do you mean by 'look around,' Nile? Belfast—the entire six counties of Ulster—are what we call a trouble spot. And looking around can get a fellow in trouble. Get your feet wet and you'll be over your head—a fellow could drown that way, if you catch my meaning."

"What's that supposed to mean? You don't want me operating on your turf?"

Topman sighed heavily and glanced at his watch. "Look, old chap, it's lunchtime. There's a canteen downstairs. Let's have a bite to eat and chat about old times."

THE MILK WAGON LUMBERED SLOWLY down Newtownards Road and stopped at the top of an incline half a block away from the brick Victorian buildings that housed military intelligence operations.

The young IRA soldier at the wheel pulled on the parking brake and reached behind the seat for a wire basket containing bottles of milk. He checked his parking spot again—a fire hydrant three meters in front and the intersection behind. Seamus had given him explicit directions. If he parked in the wrong place the mortars would fall in the wrong place. Killerbey had it figured to the last centimeter.

When he climbed down from the driver's seat, he looked like any ordinary milkman on daily rounds, with his white uniform and the milk bottles. He turned left and went around the corner until he was fifty meters away. A hedge surrounded an old school that had been bombed out several years earlier. He darted behind it and stripped off the whites. Underneath he wore civilian clothes. He left the milkman's uniform with the bottles and ran back to the street, reaching it just as Seamus and Danny drove up on the motorbikes.

Killerbey nodded for him to get on behind. The terrorists drove slowly to the intersection and stopped at the traffic light. Killerbey had the radio remote box in his hands. He clicked it on and set the dial for the frequency he wanted. Seamus turned around and smiled at Rion through the plastic visor of his helmet.

"Watch this," he said. "Those Brit bastards will eat a lunch they'll never forget."

He ground his finger into the button.

THE WIDE HALLWAYS inside the headquarters were crowded with officers and enlisted men and women, streaming for the canteen in a wing on the east side of the building. The atmosphere was lively and relaxed. The soldiers chitchatted as they headed for their noon-hour break.

Barrabas and Major Topman had just reached the first set of doors outside the canteen, when both men heard a sound familiar to all men who have seen action. A quick whistle followed by a short silence.

Very short.

In the time it took for them to hear it the building exploded.

Barrabas grabbed Topman and pushed him forward against the doorframe just as the ceiling collapsed.

The explosions didn't stop. Shock waves pounded across Barrabas and Topman, and the air was filled with flying debris that struck suddenly out of the fog of plaster and smoke.

Then there was silence.

From the canteen came the roar of a fire.

Then the screams.

Barrabas stood slowly, dust and chunks of walls falling from his arms and shoulders. He felt the sticky warmth of blood starting at the side of his face.

"Bloody doorsill saved our lives," Major Topman said, pulling himself to this feet and brushing at his uniform.

The dust was beginning to clear, and the shrieks and cries of those in pain rose to greet them. Shrill sirens screamed their alarm, and from somewhere outside the ruins of the building Barrabas heard the calls of the coming rescuers.

He headed through the drifting dust and smoke toward the moans ahead of him. He kicked something with his foot. Barrabas looked down. It was a foot. Someone else's. Still in its shoe. Its owner was missing.

His gut tightened. He'd seen it all before. Often the survivors were worse off than the dead.

Ahead of him, he saw a woman lying on her back. She was groaning and her face was obscured by blood. He knelt by her and quickly checked her injuries. Nothing broken. He lifted her and began to carry her in the direction of the shouts.

An armed trooper, the first rescuer inside, stood beside Major Topman.

"Soldier, carry this woman outside," Barrabas said, easily assuming command. The trooper took the bomb victim carefully and turned back.

"Bloodthirsty sons of bitches," Topman shrieked, clenching his fist and shaking it furiously. "Bloodthirsty sons of bitches!" It was obvious the man had lost it. Barrabas turned back into the ruins.

AN HOUR LATER, he stood back for a moment to catch his breath. His clothes were torn, and soiled with grime and blood; his hands were raw from lifting aside bits and pieces of stone and wood to get at the injured, the dead and the judgment calls in between. He had heaved a slab of masonry aside and exposed a squirming naked lump that had once been a man. It was now shorn of arms and legs, and what remained of the face was contorted in a silent scream.

Dozens of rescuers crawled through the ruins around him, and more trucks and earth-moving equipment continued to arrive outside.

A white-coated medic came to his side.

"Time out for you, sir! I want to take care of that cut on your head. We've plenty of help now. You can come on down to the medical station in the compound yard."

"I will in a moment," Barrabas said. A young woman in uniform was being helped from the shattered canteen. She was sobbing hysterically. Barrabas turned to the medic. "What's the count?"

"Thirty-seven dead so far, sir. And fifty-four wounded. It seems the dirty buggers had a milk truck around the corner with nine mortars set up inside the van. Operated by remote. It was well planned, considering the accuracy of the devices."

"Yeah, the canteen at lunchtime." He nodded toward the sobbing woman. "I'll help her down."

He walked over and put his arm around her shoulders, pulling her to him. It was all she needed. He could feel the shivers in her small body begin to subside. Her face was streaked with dirt and tears. She pressed her cheek into his side and together they walked to a part of the building that was still intact, descending to the front yard.

The place was chaos. Medical people and soldiers carried hastily bandaged wounded to the row of ambulances that lined up like taxicabs in the drive. A crowd had gathered outside the high wire fences that surrounded the compound.

As Barrabas neared the bystanders, the young woman still beside him, he scanned their sullen faces. The crowd in the predominantly Catholic neighborhood was torn between sympathy for the bombers and horror at the carnage they saw before them.

"I'm all right now, thank you." The woman pushed away from him and forced a smile as she wiped dirt and tears from her eyes. "Mr...?"

"Barrabas. Nile Barrabas."

As she walked away, Barrabas saw a familiar face staring at the scene in the compound. Mrs. O'Toole. Ellen Lorraine was beside her. The old woman locked eyes with Barrabas for a moment. Then she turned away and disappeared into the crowd.

10

Twaddell Avenue was a quiet middle-class area of wide streets and Tudor-style houses with leaded glass windows. On the opposite side of the street, half a block down, a tea shop was nestled between the butcher and the baker, in a row of stores. Billy Two and Alex Nanos took seats at a table by the window that gave them a clear view of number fifteen.

"Tea?" said Billy Two as the waitress came over.

Nanos grimaced.

They ordered coffee. The brown liquid that arrived bore a visual resemblance to coffee, but little more. They sat almost an hour watching the house. There was no movement of any kind.

"Maybe I should go in," Nanos proposed, tapping his fingers on his chest.

Billy Two looked skeptical. "Are you sure you heard the Colonel right?"

"Sure, I'm sure. Good ol' Nula McGillivry's in there right now, and she could be sitting on valuable information that we need."

"More likely she's sitting on something else," Starfoot muttered.

"Billy Two," Nanos chided him. "I'm sure she's a very nice young woman. Just got mixed up with the wrong people."

"Haven't we all," the Osage replied. "Let's take a walk first. These kinds of neighborhoods usually have alleys."

They walked to the end of the block and crossed over toward the next one. Halfway along, they found a gravel lane that led between the streets. It snaked between tightly shuttered garages and brick garden walls with wooden gates. The mercs had to estimate roughly where number fifteen was, since the backs of the houses were indistinguishable. They heard a door slam and some loud guffaws. Nanos and Starfoot ducked under the dark overhang of a garage. One of the wooden gates opened, and five young men with short military haircuts emerged into the back lane. They all wore big self-conscious smiles.

"Bang, bang, bang! Sarge didn't tell us she liked it one on top of the other!" one of them joked.

"'For queen and country, boys, queen and country.'"

The others laughed as they headed out the alley.

Nanos looked at Billy Two in disbelief. Billy Two nodded, more to himself than to Nanos.

"Sounds as if the Colonel was right on. He sure moves fast. Where does he get his info?"

"I dunno," Nanos said. He sounded a little uncertain.

"Well, Alex, you're on. Give her one of your virtuoso performances."

Nanos swallowed. "You think she still wants it? After that?" He looked in the direction of the disappearing British soldiers.

"You'll find out soon enough. Come on, let's face it. They don't have American know-how—not to mention equipment."

"True," said Alex. He still hesitated. "Should I go in the front or the back."

"Play it by ear and see what she wants."

"No, I mean into the house. The front door or the back door."

"Try the back."

Nanos stepped into the alley. He looked back at his old Indian friend. The two of them used to be paid escorts in the days before Barrabas found them. Then it was for the money. "Sure you don't want to..."

"Uh-uh. I lost it in Miami." Billy Two was enjoying this. In the old days he had been the reluctant one, with Alex "the Greek" Nanos gung ho to screw every matron with an American Express card. "Hey, Alex. Just keep rolling that lovely name over and over on your tongue. Nula McGillivry. She'll be beautiful."

Starfoot dug into the breast pocket of his jacket. He handed Alex a small square package. It was a condom.

"Where'd you get this?"

"In the toilet at the tea shop. You can never be too careful these days, Alex. Especially after the Brits have just pulled out."

Alex crossed the alley toward the back gate to number fifteen.

"She'll be beautiful, Alex!" Starfoot called after him.

Nanos crossed his fingers.

The gate was unlocked. He pushed it open and found himself inside a small, unkempt garden littered with garbage cans and broken furniture. A few spring flowers clung tenaciously to life in the stony earth along the walk. He made his way to the back door and climbed the rotting wooden steps. He knocked.

After a moment's wait the door swung inward.

A woman stood there. At least, he thought it was a woman. She filled the doorway and then some. The farther reaches of her mammoth body were lost in the distance. Her head was the size of a medicine ball, her skin puffy and white, narrowing her eyes to little slits. Her bleached-blond hair was wired into tight tiny curls that looked like electric coils. Her tiny fleshy lips, almost lost in the enormous expanse of face, wore a sour expression. The lipstick was smeared, and she was chewing on something.

"Hello," Nanos said nervously, his heart crashing down a long dark chasm and hitting the pit of his stomach. "Er, I'd like to see Nula McGillivry."

She looked at Nanos. Then her eyes moved down to his crotch. The sour expression vanished.

"Come on in," she said seductively, standing back. Her body jiggled when she moved.

Nanos moved inside with trepidation. She closed the door behind him.

"This way," she said. Her voice was soft and wispy. She led him through a hallway into the living room and carefully sat herself down on the center of a long couch. It sagged in the middle under her weight.

"Sit down," she invited him, patting the seat beside her.

Nanos chose a stuffed chair opposite.

"Nula McGillivry?" he asked uneasily. "Is she here?"

The fat lady laughed delicately. "Why, I'm Nula McGillivry. And you're an American. I just love clean-cut American guys." She winked and a tiny pink tongue appeared at the corner of her plump rosebud mouth. She patted the seat beside her invitingly.

Nanos started to sweat. Maybe, he thought, he could sweet-talk her. The silver-tongued Greek. That was it. Grab whatever information he could get from her and run.

"And what brings you to see Nula," she asked, her flesh quivering with anticipation.

Nanos coughed slightly. "Er, well I'm in Ireland looking for an old buddy who's disappeared. Someone told me that maybe you could, um, help. Information-wise, that is."

"You just come over here and sit beside Nula," Nula said, patting the couch again. "And Nula will see what she can do to help you."

Nanos swallowed and changed seats. "You see, his name is Liam O'Toole. He was on his honeymoon."

"I love honeymoons!" she swooned with half-closed eyes, moving her enormous mass up against him. It would be the best of three falls with the Michelin-tire man's twin sister, he thought.

"Yeah, well. He disappeared from his hotel. He was abducted. The last contact was a phone call he made from somewhere in Armagh. He said he was in trouble."

"Armagh, was it. I know some people in Armagh. I might be able to give you a name." She squeezed her lips together and blew him a kiss. "What can you do for me?"

Never before had the Greek's talents—and they were great—been put to such a test. He closed his eyes for a moment and thought of Atlantic City. The vision of the beauties revolving slowly on the rotating bed soothed him. He focused on the one with the nips and brought to mind the long night of passion that had preceded the arrival of the management and the Atlantic City police force. He felt his resolve stiffening.

Nula noticed. She pounced heavily.

Some minutes later Nanos was well into the thing, amazing himself with his own powers of concentration. He closed his eyes and flipped through the images of the many beautiful women he had known and loved. Except for a few tactile differences the situations were the same. He was riding her, fast and hot.

Nula McGillivry groaned and shuddered with ecstasy.

"Oh, yes, ooh."

"What have you got for me, baby? Who do you know in Armagh?" Although he was having the required success in the matter at hand, he wanted to get it over with.

"Ohhh, yesss, I'll tell you everything. Everything!"

"Come on, baby. Let's have it. Tell Alex everything you know." Check this out, Billy Two, he thought as he performed. The Greek's in top form.

"Oh, yesss."

Alex stopped.

"Don't stop. Please don't stop."

"Who's your friend in Armagh."

"Oh, please. Not now. I'll tell you everything. Please keep going, keep going."

"I gotta know, baby."

Nula squirmed breathlessly. "Darby O'Goole. He knows everything that goes on in Armagh. Now please, please keep going."

Alex didn't move. "Where do I find him?"

"In Kelligro. He's priest there. For crissake, keep going!"

Suddenly Alex had the sensation of being spied on. He looked around. On the other side of the window at the back of the room, the big laughing face of Billy Two stared in.

Nanos's resolve vanished. It was time to pull out. He grabbed his pants and struggled into them.

A look of pure horror crossed Nula McGillivry's face. "What are you doing? Please don't leave me like this!"

Nanos grabbed his jacket and headed for the back door. "Great time, babe. I'll be seeing ya. Thanks for the dope on O'Goole."

Her plaintive wails followed him out the back door. "Where are you going? Get back here right now! How dare—"

He slammed the door as he went out. In the tattered little garden, Billy Two was waiting, the big smile still in place.

"Don't even think it, you spying son of a bitch." Alex stormed angrily toward the gate to the alley.

"Hey, Alex. You were in great form."

Nanos stopped. His face lit up. "Yeah. I was, wasn't I? And even better, I got the berries. Some priest named Darby O'Goole in a place called Kelligro."

AT DUSK, Barrabas was sitting in the back of a big black taxi with Lee Hatton. They were so far north, night came early and quickly. Overhead the sky was dark, but in the west a long white line marked what remained of the day. The eerie half-light from the last departing rays of sun washed across Belfast.

The rendezvous of the mercs at the Great Boar had given Barrabas enough to work with for the next day. Nate Beck had done his computer work well. O'Toole's telephone call had come from a pay phone in the countryside of County Armagh—just outside Kelligro. It was probably no coincidence that Darby O'Goole, the name Nanos had obtained from Nula McGillivry, happened to be the parish priest in that village. Bits and pieces of the puzzle were beginning to fit together.

Bishop had managed to locate a five-speed streamlined Toyota van to get them around. They'd start their excursion to see the parish priest first thing in the morning. There was one last detail to take care of: guns.

The taxi stopped on a deserted shopping street near city hall.

"Ya won't be staying out long around here, will ya? Not in this neighborhood," the taxi driver said, turning around from the front seat to warn them.

"We'll be fine." Barrabas gave him the money, and he and Lee stepped onto the sidewalk.

Lee drew in her breath and pulled her coat around her. "Nippy for spring," she commented.

"How'd you know about this guy?" Barrabas asked. They turned east and walked against the wind.

"I was in on an investigation of some Irish-American benevolent association that was running guns. We're going to see their Ulster sales rep. We let the FBI arrest the American end of the arrangement, but I figured that by now the guy here would have another supplier. He does. Here it is."

She stopped outside a cheap jewelry store, the place that sold electroplated Forever bands studded with real zircons. Even so, the plate-glass windows were covered with heavy grilles. Hatton stuck her hand through an opening and rapped on the door.

A gray-haired man with round wire glasses and a preoccupied air came to the door and opened the grille about a foot. "Come on—make it fast. Hello, Dr. Hatton. I presume you're the interested gentleman," he said, looking at Barrabas when they were inside. "Don't bother introducing yourself. We don't need names around here. Just cash. They're right over here."

The glass counter that displayed the large selection of inexpensive wedding rings was spread with a collection of Ingram MAC-10 submachine guns and parts for them.

"It's the kind of gun you can tie a rope around, lower into a room via the window and let rip. It'll kill everyone present. A low-class weapon, really." He sounded a little apologetic, but flashed a quick salesman's smile. "Nevertheless, it does do the job. And it's all I've got in stock, as I told Dr. Hatton earlier today."

Barrabas couldn't help laughing when he picked up the gun. The ridiculous little tin box with the peashooter stuck out of one end was not his preferred weapon. The big ammo, .45 or .380, fired at twelve hundred rounds a minute and traveled at eight hundred and fifty feet a second. Thirty shells in three seconds. The weapon wasn't very accurate, but at those speeds who cared.

"How many you got?"

"Three now. In another hour, six."

Lee Hatton picked up a metal plate with stampings on it. "This is one of our Ingrams. To beat the gun laws, one of the manufacturers broke the receivers in the MAC-10s to sell them as wall ornaments. In the package came an easy instruction book telling you how to turn this into a working receiver and convert it to full auto at the same time."

"Yes, it was the 'Beat the Heat' model, if I recall," the store owner told him, looking over the tops of the wire-rim glasses at the assembled MAC in his hand. "Eventually the federal authorities caught on to that little scam, too. I bought up the remainder of the stock and, ahem—" he looked grimly at Hatton "—had it shipped here. But we won't go into that."

"The receivers hold the firing mechanism. How do I know these are put together the right way?" Barrabas said. "I don't want to find out at the wrong time."

"Come with me." Almost indignantly, the jeweler dashed from behind the counter and walked to the back of the store, motioning for Barrabas and Lee to follow.

On the other side of a curtain and past a barrier of shipping crates was the test area. At the end of a hundred-foot gallery, three mannequins that had once been used to display necklaces out in the shop stood in a row.

The gray-haired jeweler pointed the MAC in the general direction of one of them and let go. The mannequin shattered into a thousand plaster bits. He handed the gun to Barrabas.

"Go ahead."

Barrabas took it and lined himself up with the second mannequin. The same thing happened when he pulled the trigger.

"Now try this one," the dealer said, taking the MAC from his hands and handing him one with a silencer.

"Lee." Barrabas handed the SMG to her.

Hatton aimed, and the third mannequin evaporated. The noise was no louder than an electric fan.

Barrabas pulled a wad of bills out of his breast pocket. "How much?"

"Six thousand. Dollars."

"They sell for two hundred in the States."

"Then buy them in the States." The jeweler counted the money Barrabas handed him and looked up. "And get them into the country your own bloody self."

"Take care of the rest of them, Lee." Barrabas stuck one of the MACs into a pouch sewn inside the lining of his jacket, along with a couple of magazines, and started for the front door.

"Sure. Are you off somewhere?"

"I want to see Major Topman again. I wasn't finished with him when those mortars hit today. It looks like we've narrowed down our search to Armagh and the southern border of Ulster. I want to find out what he knows about the IRA organization in that area."

OUTSIDE THE JEWELRY STORE Barrabas turned north onto Victoria Street to cross the Lagan River at Bridge End. It was dark now, and the downtown area was empty. The night was slightly misty, and a damp chill filled the air. The yellow lights glowed wickedly along the shiny wet surfaces of the streets.

He was aware of the sound of a motor in the distance behind him. A second later, headlights from an approaching vehicle threw his shadow ahead of him on the pavement. He turned when he heard the vehicle slow.

It was a Land Rover with the distinctive markings of the Royal Ulster Constabulary. It pulled to the curb, and a deep Irish voice shouted from the window, "Hold it there, fella!"

With practiced precision, four police swarmed from the Rover and fanned around Barrabas.

"Can we have your identification, if you please."
The leader was a big overweight man with a tiny mustache.

Barrabas flicked his steel blue eyes over the constables, sizing them up for trouble. Their belts were heavy with billy sticks, hand radios and thick notebooks filled with summonses. These were the kind of men who joined the police as an excuse to throw their weight around. The worst. He handed the man his passport.

"Well, well," the head constable said, flipping through it. "Claims 'e's an American. And what might you be doing out on these streets at this time of night?"

"I didn't know there was a law against it."

"Oh, there's laws agin all sorts of things in Belfast, my man. We don't get a lot of tourists from America here, and those we do get aren't usually found walking these streets at night when they should be safe in their hotel rooms. Perhaps you'll get into the jeep and come on down to the station, where we can get this straightened out."

Barrabas felt the weight of the MAC in his jacket. If he cooperated—played the dumb American out for an evening walk—there was a possibility they might not search him. If they found the MAC, there'd be serious trouble.

"I have a meeting with Major Topman at military intelligence. He's an old friend."

The constable started to laugh. "Ho-ho! He's a friend of the Major's, is he?" He looked around at the other policemen, waiting for them to share in the joke.

A couple of them smiled self-consciously. "Search him, boys."

Barrabas stepped back and to the side, ready to take out the short paunchy officer to his right, when the billy stick whacked down hard on the back of his head. He barely retained consciousness as his legs went weak. Before he collapsed they were on him, frisking him and jerking the MAC out of its hiding place.

"Right, lads. Put on the cuffs and throw him in back. Bloody Yanks. Coming over here to play savior with their arms and money for the IRA!"

11

By the time the Land Rover arrived at the Strand Road police station Barrabas had regained his strength. It was too late to put it to any use, though. His hands were cuffed so tightly the circulation was cut off. And the back of his head felt like a bruised melon. That was twice today. He had a jagged cut near his temple from the mortar explosions earlier.

He was led roughly into the station, where the head constable threw the MAC onto the night sergeant's desk. "Says 'e's a friend of Major Topman's." He laughed. "Friends like this I'd hardly be thinking the Major is needing."

"Take him back there," the sergeant told the police, narrowing his eyes and looking Barrabas up and down. He picked up the American passport and began flipping through it.

Barrabas was pushed into a brightly lit room with cinder-block walls and a cold cement floor. There were three chairs. The room was designed for a specific function, but the Colonel didn't have time to think about it. The policeman behind him spun him around, and Barrabas felt the force of a fist in his gut just before he fell against the wall. His legs gave out and he slipped slowly to the floor.

Rough hands grabbed him and threw him onto one of the chairs. He felt their fists slap into the bone just behind his ears as the men cursed him. They were experts. This kind of physical punishment left no telltale marks on the body.

His ears were ringing and his head spun with pain. Instinctively he tried to throw himself sideways and away from the pummeling fists, but they held him tight. He felt a hand come down on the crown of his head and jab down, slapping his chin into his sternum until he felt his teeth crushing and his vertebrae grind. Then the hands moved to his shoulder and pushed. The pain under his rib cage was excruciating as he was forced to bend in half. He felt the last thread of consciousness drifting away to escape the agony that wracked his body. He made no sound.

Dimly he heard a voice shouting questions about the IRA. They wanted to know his real name, where was he going, who was he trying to see.

"We've got a tough one here," one of his torturers remarked.

His chair was moved and its back pushed against the cinder-block wall. A big hand closed over the top of his head and pushed it back. He felt the solid punches of closed fists smashing into the underside of his chin, slamming the back of his head against the wall. His mouth filled with blood, bile and chips of tooth.

Repeatedly loud voices shouted into both ears. The questions and curses filtered through the haze of pain and registered vaguely. The assault on his head stopped, but they weren't finished. Two policemen each grabbed one of his knees and began to pull in opposite directions. A groan broke off in his throat as the pain in his hip sockets jolted upward through his body.

Suddenly it stopped. As the pain ebbed, he felt nauseous and weak. He fought against it, trying to focus his vision. He wanted to see the faces of the men who were doing this to him. He wanted to remember them. He was going to come back for them someday.

He shook his head to clear it. The blows behind his ears had disoriented him. He struggled against a growing dizziness, but felt himself falling to one side. He hit the floor with a thud. The cold floor pressed against his cheek felt good. Against the wall, heating ducts ran upward to the ceiling. He felt the heat on his back. It felt good, too. A body in terrible pain makes do.

The Royal Ulster Constabulary, however, weren't finished, it seemed. He heard something and opened his eyes. Footsteps scuffled on the cement floor and big leather boots stopped inches from his face. He heard the man who stood above him hork and spit. The great gob landed on his face, just beside his mouth.

"Hey, Kevin!" The man shouted. "He likes that, 'e does."

A second man walked over. "He does, does 'e? Well, now, I don't mind obligin' him." The second man horked and spat.

Barrabas closed his eyes and felt the warm gob slide down his cheek. He heard the man talking again.

"Maybe it's time for the plastic bags," one of them said.

"I think so. He should be a mite softer now. Clean his face off. I'll get them."

He felt a towel wipe the spittle across his mouth. A policeman chuckled goonishly. Barrabas was lifted by his collar, and he opened his eyes just in time to see a green garbage bag pulled down over his head.

He reacted, throwing his legs forward to kick the policeman who was holding his collar, and twisting away from the one who had the bag.

"Stop it! Immediately!" a commanding voice shouted harshly.

The bag was jerked away from his head, and he felt hands rushing to unlock the handcuffs and pull him to his feet. When he looked, Barrabas saw the desk sergeant standing with his old friend Major Topman.

"I'm afraid there's been a terrible mistake here, old chap," Topman said. "Are you all right?"

Barrabas shook his hands to get the blood back in them and wiped the spit from his lips with his sleeve.

"Nope."

Slowly, painfully, he felt his ribs. Topman and the desk sergeant were concerned and a little frightened. Barrabas felt himself tilt to one side, his sense of balance distorted by the beating. He ordered himself to straighten up. His body obeyed.

"I feel terrible about this, Nile. When they found the gun they thought you were out to assassinate me. I'm at the top of the IRA list, as I've told you. Terribly sorry, old chap."

"Get me out of here," Barrabas said grimly.

"Absolutely. Sergeant, have this man's possessions returned to him."

"Right away, Major."

The two torturers stood back with sullen looks, half pissed that the fun and games were over and half frightened of anticipated reprisals.

"And these two?" Barrabas growled. He jerked his thumb at them, his lip curling spontaneously in a sneer.

"I assure you, Mr. Barrabas, these two men will be disciplined to the fullest extent possible under police regulations."

"Sure."

Barrabas walked toward the door, with Topman on his right and the two torturers to his left. He waited until he was directly in front of them. He swung fast as smoke, driving his right hand into the gut of the man on the left and crossing over to hurtle his left fist into number two's face.

"Stop it! Stop it now." Topman and the sergeant came between the men and Barrabas, pushing them apart.

The first man grunted, too breathless to tell them how much it hurt. The second one screamed and held his face. Blood dribbled from the man's nose and lips.

Barrabas pushed Topman and the sergeant aside.

A few minutes later, in the back of Major Topman's chauffeur-driven car, the British army officer apologized profusely.

"These tactics are impolite, to say the least, and indeed, sometimes the local police do show a bit too much enthusiasm, but considering the situation here,

Nile, it's necessary. You saw earlier today the kind of thing the enemy is capable of.''

"The problem is that in a civil war like this one, after so many years of bloodshed both sides forget what they're fighting for, and it's impossible to say what's right and what's wrong. The laws of civilization don't apply. Life is nasty and brutish, and ultimately both sides lose.''

"Well, really, Nile. You're beginning to sound like a moralist. We've both been at this long enough to know it's just another job. Not the most pleasant, perhaps. But we're as human as those who keep their hands clean.''

"Are there clean hands in Ireland?''

"Probably not.'' Topman reached inside his long officer's coat and withdrew Barrabas's MAC. "I imagine you got this from that jeweler over near city hall. I should have known he'd be back in business.'' He handed it to the Colonel, along with the spare mags. "The only reason I'm giving it back is that regardless of the target, you'll be doing me a favor.''

Barrabas slipped the MAC back inside his jacket. "What do you know about IRA activity in Armagh?''

Topman nodded approvingly. "I figured you'd have your search narrowed down by now. You amaze me, Nile. If I had one other officer like you, we'd have these bastards beat. As for Armagh, that's one of our weak areas. We're currently taking initiatives there. We know the IRA are very active. They have safe houses, and probably some bomb factories in the area. The operation you saw today—this man Simon

McVaghey—we hope he'll lead us to their next target before they carry the plan through."

"What about someone named Darby O'Goole? A priest."

Topman looked at Barrabas, unable to conceal his surprise. "Astonishing. I won't ask you where you got that piece of information. It took us years. We suspect O'Goole of harboring nationalist sympathies. And as a man of the cloth, he's been giving last rites and saying funeral masses for a number of IRA dead."

The car stopped in front of Barrabas's hotel.

Topman paused, studying Barrabas intensely. "The informer on Tom Murphy—you wanted to know his name earlier today. It was a man named Seamus Killerbey. I had the reports checked after you left. Your friend Liam O'Toole belonged to the same IRA cell."

"Where can I find Killerbey?"

"Well, if you can, Nile, you're a better man than I. He's IRA, hard-core, despite the information in our files. Right now he's underground. He's a tricky bastard. The mortar attack today had his hallmark."

"If I find him, I'll let you know."

"That would be splendid, old chap. And Nile, the word is that the IRA are engaged in a spring offensive—revenge for the death of Terry McHugh, who was gunned down by the British army last week. It's going to be long and bloody. The mortar attack today was only the beginning. We know they've something else in the planning stage. Something far worse. That's all I've got to give you on it at the moment. That and some advice—be careful."

The British major smiled. "Terribly sorry about the misunderstanding."

Barrabas got out.

Topman stuck his head from the window just before the car drove off. "And as far as finding your friend goes, you're on the right track. Good luck, Nile!"

The car vanished down the dark wet street.

ONE MOMENT THE STREET WAS EMPTY, and the next, four RUC Land Rovers poured around the corner and jerked to a halt outside a small brick row house. Police officers poured out and fanned around the doors and windows.

Half a dozen raced to the front door. They didn't knock. The butts of heavy rifles splintered the wood, crumbling the door into bits and pieces in the front hall.

A short elderly man holding a newspaper, and his tiny gray-haired wife, stood by a stairway, their faces stunned with fear. Behind them a television blared. Simon McVaghey stood up from the couch with a nervous smile on his face. As the police moved into the house, he eagerly searched their faces for a friendly smile.

But it wasn't the same as at the police station, where they told him they were his friends and offered him ten pounds sterling to do them a favor.

"We are acting on information that arms and ammunition are hidden in this house by suspected IRA terrorists," a bullying officer roared at Simon McVaghey's amazed parents. "Search the house!"

The RUC troopers stormed upstairs.

"You there—what's your name?" The officer pointed at McVaghey. The old couple were hustled roughly against a wall with their hands up.

"Get over there, between those two and the door," the simpleton was told. Meekly he obeyed.

Upstairs, four policemen rushed straight into McVaghey's bedroom, momentarily startled by what they saw. The room was full of stuffed animals and wooden toys. It was like a child's room. The first policeman in ripped open the top drawer of the dresser and found the cigarette package at the bottom. Exactly where McVaghey had been told to put it. He pushed up the inner package. The three .45 bullets glinted against the foil wrap.

"Found it, Captain!" The officer shouted from the top of the stairs. "In the son's bedroom."

"B-b-but that's impossible," the old man stuttered. "My son is . . . he's not quite right!" His wife looked from her husband to the captain and back again. She was on the verge of total collapse.

Another policeman leaned close to Simon McVaghey, who watched the proceedings, puzzled. The policemen had told him they would come, but he hadn't imagined it would be like this. Simon McVaghey trembled in confusion. He'd forgotten what he was to do.

"Better make your run for it now, laddy," the policeman whispered softly. He jerked his head toward the front door.

McVaghey remembered. With a last doubtful backward glance, he flung himself through the doorway and raced down the sidewalk to the street.

"'E's escaping!" one of the police shouted. Several raced after the fleeing man, their feet pounding heavily down the pavement, until the men were lost from sight.

12

Alex Nanos and Geoff Bishop sat in a small maroon Renault in the square of Kelligro, the little Ulster village a few miles from the border of the Irish Republic. Neither man had a great deal to say to the other at the best of times. And increasingly, it seemed, Barrabas was putting them together on assignments. For two hours they sat without a word passing between them.

From their vantage point they had a clear view of a small stone twelfth-century church and the parish house next door. According to the information the mercs had obtained, it was the home of the IRA sympathizer Father Darby O'Goole.

Bishop looked at his watch. Eleven o'clock.

"Time to report to the Colonel."

Nanos grunted without taking his eyes off the church and the parish house.

Bishop reached under the dashboard and flicked the button on the two-way radio secreted there. The day before he had spent the afternoon equipping the mercs with hardware and transportation. He coiled the transmitter cord around his arm to hide it and carefully cupped the mouthpiece in his hand as he held it to his lips. Some mild static came from the receiver. Then he heard Barrabas's voice.

Bishop spoke softly. "All we've seen is a half-dozen old ladies go into the house about half an hour ago, Colonel."

Several blocks away, the other mercs waited in a brown Toyota van. Lee Hatton sat at the wheel, Nate Beck and Billy Two in back. Barrabas operated the radio from the passenger seat.

"Okay, Geoff. We could be sitting around for days, and we don't have that kind of time. I'm going to pay a visit. You two hold tight until further notice. Over and out."

"Next stop Father Darby O'Goole?" Lee Hatton asked.

Barrabas nodded. "Starfoot, you come in with me."

"How are you going to do this?" Nate Beck asked.

"Well, I figure it's going to take a long time for us to find them. So we'll let them come to us, instead."

"This way they'll sure know where to look," Nate said with a sigh.

"Whoever 'they' are," Hatton added.

She put the van in gear and drove them to the parish house. It had a thatched roof and shuttered casement windows. Barrabas and Starfoot looked warily at the old stone church beside them, and the graveyard full of ancient tombstones carved in Celtic crosses and inscribed in Gaelic.

"Sure is old," Billy Two commented.

They walked up to the low stoop in front of the door and knocked. A woman in a black-and-white maid's uniform opened the door almost immediately, as if she had been expecting someone. Her welcoming eyes suddenly clouded over at the sight of two big men.

"We have to see Father O'Goole," Barrabas told her.

"Oh, I'm terribly sorry, he's busy. Did you make an appointment?"

Barrabas pushed the door open and walked inside, with Billy Two right behind him. The maid was indignant.

"Why, you can't just barge in here like that. How dare you—"

"We don't need an appointment. We just need to see Father O'Goole. Now."

"Why, I'll have the village constable after you—"

She was interrupted when sliding doors on one side of the hallway opened. A tall, middle-aged man in a priest's cassock and collar stood imposingly at the entrance to a sitting room. The gray hair at his temples and his wide shoulders lent him an impressive air. Behind him, frozen in midconversation on settees around a small table, sat six women holding teacups.

"I'm Father O'Goole," the priest said in a deep, firm voice, eyeing Barrabas and Billy Two. "Can I help you?"

"We're looking for someone," Barrabas told him. "I have a feeling you can help us."

"And who might that be?" O'Goole demanded.

"Liam O'Toole."

IN THE RENAULT, half a block away, Bishop and Nanos, both stiff from the long hours of inactivity, shifted in their seats. They watched the Toyota van drive up and Barrabas go into the house with Billy Two.

Suddenly Bishop started and sat up straighter.

"Alex, look at that."

"I see, I see," the Greek answered, leaning closer to the windshield. Three men were making their way behind the church and through the tombstones in the ancient graveyard, heading for the back of the parish house. "Better get on the blower to Nate and Hatton." He reached for the door handle and pulled the MAC-10 out of his jacket.

"Hey, where are you going?" Bishop demanded.

"I'm not just going to sit here and watch while the Colonel and Billy Two are in there being set up."

Bishop shook his head emphatically. "Uh-uh. Colonel said to stay put. So we stay put."

"Bishop, you can stick it where the moon don't shine. I take orders from the Colonel, not from you."

"Right. And the Colonel said stay put."

"Yeah? With three guys heading in there?"

"I just have a feeling we're more useful staying right where we are."

Bishop reached under the dashboard for the radio.

FOR A MOMENT the priest hesitated. He looked quickly behind him at the ladies, who watched the proceedings with considerable interest. It was not every day that a white-haired American and an Indian turned up in Kelligro.

"We can speak for a moment in my study. But as you can see, I am already engaged. These good Catholic women are involved in fund-raising for some parish activities. I don't have a lot of time.''

He closed the doors behind him and led them past the livid maid into a small office with a big crucifix on the wall.

''Now perhaps you could tell me who you are and what you want.''

Barrabas nailed him with steel eyes. Darby O'Goole met his stare.

''Nile Barrabas. And this is Billy Starfoot.''

O'Goole's face remained impassive. ''And who is it you're looking for?''

''Liam O'Toole.''

The priest furrowed his brow in thought. Then he shook his head. ''I'm afraid I don't recognize the name.''

''He called a friend in New York on Tuesday and said he was in trouble. He never finished the call. It was traced to a phone booth in the countryside not far from here.''

''I'm sorry, but it doesn't mean a thing to me.''

''Doesn't make much sense to us, either.''

At that moment the phone on the priest's desk rang. He answered it and listened for a few seconds. A worried look suddenly shadowed his face, and he glanced quickly at his two unexpected visitors.

''All right,'' O'Goole said into the phone. ''I'll take care of it shortly.'' He turned to Barrabas and Billy Two. ''Gentlemen,'' he said expansively. ''I'm very, very busy. And I'm sorry I can't help you. I don't know of any Liam O'Toole.'' He moved toward the door to show them out.

"What about Seamus Killerbey?" Barrabas asked.

This time the priest reacted—barely, but enough to let Barrabas know the name had registered.

"I'm sorry. I'm not familiar with that name, either." He paused at the door, considering whether to say anything more. Then he asked, "Why have you come to me? Who told you I could help you?"

"I heard you know just about everything that goes on in Armagh."

Father O'Goole smiled modestly. "I am but a simple man of God." He ushered them into the hallway and opened the front door.

"Yeah, so am I. Guess we'll check out that phone booth our friend made the call from," Barrabas said, looking straight at Father O'Goole. Billy Two followed him out the door with a final stare at the priest's face.

The door closed heavily behind them.

In the house, Father O'Goole stood by the closed door, thinking. The maid came into the hall from the back of the house.

"Where are they?" O'Goole asked her.

"In the kitchen, Father."

"It seems everyone is showing up this morning," he said grimly. He hurried past her, his long black robes flying behind him.

In the kitchen, two men in faded overalls sipped from mugs. A third sat at the table, drawing patterns with his finger in some spilled coffee on the wooden surface. He looked up and grinned stupidly when Father O'Goole entered the room.

"And who might this be?" O'Goole demanded.

The two IRA men barely looked up from their tea.

"'E's on the lam from the cops, 'e is," said one. "'E says 'e's with one of the Strand cells in Belfast. The cops raided 'is 'ome and found some ammo."

The priest narrowed his eyes and surveyed McVaghey. The man didn't look much like IRA material. One of the disadvantages to cell organization was that it was easy for the police to slip in their agents. It was impossible for a truly centralized chain of command to exist.

"You've confirmed this?" O'Goole asked.

The two IRA men nodded. "We had word of the police raid before 'e turned up. Caused a bit of a commotion in the neighborhood, it did."

Grudgingly the priest nodded. "Then let's get him out of here and to the safe house. We have a bigger problem to worry about now."

"And what might that be?" one of the Irishmen asked, tipping his cup to drain it.

"One man. And I have the feeling he'll be more trouble to us than the constabulary and the British army combined."

Then he left the kitchen and walked quickly back to his study, where he picked up the telephone and dialed a number. He waited as it rang.

"Seamus? It's Darby O'Goole."

The IRA leader's merry voice came over the line. "And what can we do for you now, Father?"

"What I warned you might happen has happened. Liam O'Toole's friends just came looking for him. This American, Nile Barrabas, is on our trail. I'm coming out there. But in the meantime, they're on their way to the crossroads O'Toole telephoned from when you allowed him to escape. Perhaps you should send some of your men out there. These Americans must be eliminated. Immediately. Before it's too late."

"THEY SURE AS HELL KNOW we're around now," Billy Two said with a grin as the two mercs walked back to the Toyota van. "How long you figure till they come for us?"

"Not long," Barrabas said. "Not if we're on the right track."

"I think we are. Did you see the look in the good Father's eyes when you mentioned Killerbey's name?"

"Yup."

They climbed into the van.

"That was fast." Lee Hatton seemed surprised to see them. She told them what Bishop and Nanos had seen.

"We had just about decided to come in after you," Nate Beck said.

Barrabas nodded. "There was a phone call, and then we were ushered out abruptly. Major Topman warned me something was going on. The IRA are supposed to be planning a spring offensive. It looks as if we've landed right in the middle of it. Where's that telephone booth, Nate?"

Beck leaned forward from the back seat with a folded map in his hands. He showed Barrabas a spot marked ten kilometers outside the village.

Barrabas handed the map to Lee Hatton. "Take me there. I want Bishop and Nanos to follow at a safe distance." Once again he reached for the two-way radio.

Billy Two sighed. "Yeah. I always feel better when there's some backup," he commented to Nate Beck.

"Sure. Two real good fighters."

"Yeah." The Indian looked momentarily doubtful. "When they're not at each other's throats."

THE ROAD OUT OF KELLIGRO led through rolling farmland, emerald green from spring rains. It took about ten minutes for the Toyota to reach the spot where a gravel road turned onto the pavement. On one side of the paved road, an old stone building with a thatched roof housed a restaurant and a little store that stocked souvenirs for the summer tourist traffic. Hatton pulled the van into the parking lot. The telephone booth stood near the road.

The mercs got out. The late-morning sun was warm, and the countryside quiet and incongruously peaceful. The face of a shopkeeper appeared at the window of the little store, then disappeared. The Colonel and the three SOBs stared at the telephone booth.

The glass in one of the side panels had been shattered into a spider's web. At the center was a small round hole.

"Bullet," Barrabas said. He opened the door and stepped inside.

The telephone receiver hung uselessly at the end of its cord. He lifted it up. It had been shattered. Then he looked at the floor.

"Blood," Hatton said. She stood behind him and spoke over his shoulder.

He stepped out. The four mercs stood around uncomfortably, no one saying anything. Finally Barrabas spoke.

"The authorities still haven't found a body."

No one needed to say that there was still a chance that O'Toole was alive, or that they wouldn't stop until they had found their former comrade, dead or alive.

"There'll be hell to pay," said Billy Two.

Barrabas looked at the empty windows of the shop and restaurant. "Wait here. I'm going to talk to the owners of this place."

He crossed the parking lot and pulled open the flimsy wooden door of the restaurant. A bell jingled on a cord as he stepped inside, and almost immediately a curly haired, heavy-set man entered through the swinging door that led from the kitchen. He stood behind the counter, near the cash register.

"Are you the owner?" Barrabas asked.

"That I am," the man said somewhat defensively. "And what can I do to help you?"

"How long has the phone been out of order?"

The man replied slowly, guarding his words. "Oh, about a week, I'd say. I have one in the back, if you're in need of it."

Barrabas shook his head. "It looks like it's been shot up."

The shopkeeper's eyes were wary. "That I cannot say." He shrugged.

"Have you had a look at it?"

"No, I canna say I have, mister. Would you be from the telephone company, perhaps?"

"No. I'm from America. And I don't have time for pissing around. I want to know what happened out there last Tuesday morning."

"Well, now, nothing happened that I'm aware of."

"Then why is there dried blood on the floor of the phone booth and a bullet hole in the glass?"

The shopkeeper shifted uncomfortably. His eyes flicked over Barrabas's shoulders and out the windows to the parking lot. The Colonel heard the sound of a vehicle screeching quickly off the pavement onto the gravel. He turned around and saw a white van brake abruptly across the entrance of the parking lot.

HATTON, BECK AND STARFOOT swung around, pulling the MAC-10s from their jackets as the rear doors flung open. Masked men holding automatic rifles poured out.

Lee Hatton saw them coming first, but by then the white van was almost on top of them.

"Billy!" She shouted a warning to the Indian, who stood near the phone booth. She grabbed Nate Beck and pulled him to cover behind the Toyota. Starfoot dived into a shallow ditch at the edge of the road.

Automatic-rifle fire ripped the peaceful Irish morning in half. The IRA bullets chunged into the Toyota as Hatton and Beck disappeared from sight. Another gunman took aim at the disappearing Osage warrior. Billy Two yelped as he hit the ditch. He looked at his foot. A bullet had bitten through the side of his shoe. He could see bare skin. Then the skin started to bleed.

"Big mistake," he muttered. "Now you got one mad Injun on your mickey hands." He flopped over on his belly, pulling his MAC from underneath him and aiming it on the road.

Someone in the white van shouted orders as Nate Beck ran along the side of the Toyota toward the front. Before he got there, one of the attackers made a suicide run around the SOBs' vehicle to gun down the two hiding mercs.

Bad idea.

Beck pulled the trigger. The MAC jerked almost uncontrollably in his hands as it sowed its bloody seeds up the IRA man's chest before taking out the Toyota's side mirror. Beck looked at the remains of the mirror.

"Shit," he cursed. "We'll have to pay for that." His opponent fell, face first, onto the pavement and stayed there.

On the other side, another attacker spun around to get Hatton, who was crouched behind the rear wheel.

Billy Two opened up from the ditch. The little tin box almost pulled from his hands as it spun rounds in a line up the man's body from his crotch to his shoulder. The .038 stopped him dead in his tracks.

Mainly dead. He fell against the Toyota with one hand out to hold on. His body slid down the side of the van, leaving a slick red trail.

Bullets kept flying from Billy Two's MAC as the strong recoil pulled it up and to the left. The metal projectiles tore through the open rear door of the white van. Below the door, Starfoot could see a man's legs from the knees down.

He pulled down the autorifle to take out his opponent's kneecaps.

It wasn't necessary.

One of the bullet holes in the van door spouted a red fountain. The man fell backward as his legs wavered, and his arms flew wide, hurtling his weapon across the gravel road.

A momentary calm returned to the Irish morning as the stalemated enemies played a game called Who Goes First?

13

Barrabas crossed to the door in two long strides. His hand reached into his jacket to pull out the deadly SMG. He heard the shopkeeper move behind him and he turned.

The man was pulling a long-barreled handgun from a drawer under the counter. Both men's eyes flashed with deadly hatred in the race to kill.

Barrabas won.

He lifted the MAC-10 and squeezed. The small metal box gurgled its big payload, wiping a gore line up the man's chest and blowing his skull into poker chips and porridge. The gun clattered onto the keys of the cash register. The bell rang and the cash drawer swung out, socking the dead man in the paunch. The body keeled over and thudded heavily on the floor behind the counter.

Outside the shooting had already started.

Hatton and Beck crouched behind the Toyota in a standoff with the attackers. There was a body lying in the parking lot. Billy Two was nowhere to be seen. Then Barrabas saw the bullets come from the ditch and slam into an IRA man as he swung around the van.

The Colonel opened the door and whipped across the parking lot toward the cover of the Toyota. Five meters from it he pitched himself forward in a head-first, Pete Rose first-base slide. He threw his arms out in front of him and led with the MAC. As he slid toward the Toyota, he squeezed the trigger.

Barrabas didn't bother to count the feet on the far side of the white van as he fired. His muscles strained to hold the MAC down as a half-dozen rounds raked the ground. He released the trigger almost immediately. He was firing under the Toyota, as well as under the attackers' vehicle, and the virtually uncontrollable recoil from the MAC would have ricocheted the next rounds off the undercarriage.

He stopped sliding and flipped in a fast roll until he came up beside Hatton, covered by the Toyota's rear wheel. Someone was screaming in pain on the other side of the white van.

"You got at least one," Hatton said grimly.

Barrabas couldn't help smiling as he picked himself up. "How many to go?"

Hatton shrugged. "One? Maybe two. I wouldn't mind getting a shot in myself."

Suddenly they heard the door of the white van slam shut and the motor roar. The van pulled forward, braked with a screech and backed up, slamming into the side of the Toyota.

"Stop them," Barrabas shouted to Hatton and Beck. "I want prisoners."

The white van surged forward again. One of the IRA attackers was still outside, hobbling on one foot as blood gushed out of a raw wound below his knee.

He waved his hands and ran in front of the van, begging his buddies to stop.

They didn't.

He screamed horribly as he came face-to-face with the big white truth.

The van hit him head on and kept rolling. It lurched as the wheels went over his body. There was the sickening sound of bones cracking and breaking.

Billy Two jumped up from his ditch and pumped .038s in a line across the side of the van's front door at about leg level. The vehicle fishtailed as it turned east onto the gravel road, the rear doors flying open and shut. Barrabas ran from cover and fired his MAC at the rear tires.

The little killing machine just didn't have it in the accuracy sweepstakes.

Hatton was already at the wheel of the Toyota, when they heard the sound of another vehicle, approaching from the west. It was the maroon Renault.

Nanos and Bishop saw the turmoil at the crossroads restaurant just as the white van swerved onto the road and headed off.

Nanos floored it.

The little French car kicked up dust as it zipped by the other mercs and closed in on the escaping van. A man leaned out the passenger window and started firing.

The bullets chunged against the hood and roof of the Renault, and a headlight exploded. Nanos veered left and pulled the car up within a few feet of the swinging rear doors. The gunman pulled his head in the window and turned in his seat to fire out the back way.

"How're we going to do this?" Nanos asked, maintaining an even distance from the rear of the van. The doors had swung closed, momentarily affording them some cover.

"This way," Bishop said between clenched teeth. He pulled his legs up onto the seat and stuck most of his body out the window. Holding the MAC in his left hand, he aimed at the rear of the white van, waiting for the doors to swing open again.

They did.

Bishop emptied a round at the passenger's seat. The man sitting in it bucked and twisted as the bullets tore through him. The van's windshield exploded. Bishop dropped back inside the car.

"Now pull up beside the driver."

Nanos jerked the car sideways and began to overtake the van. The driver saw them coming and steered left, pushing them off the road. The Greek jerked the steering wheel sharply to the right.

"What the hell! The headlight's already gone!" Nanos yelled, his wild eyes glowing.

The Renault bashed into the side of the van, causing it to fishtail on the gravel. Nanos gripped the steering wheel to the car on the road. He gave it some more gas and pushed until the front bumper was just behind the van's front door. The escaping driver threw them a panicked backward glance and veered left again.

"Never look back!" Alex shouted hoarsely through the windshield. "'Cause someone's gaining on you."

He jerked the steering wheel sharp right again and bashed in the side of the van, forcing it over. He gave the car more gas. The Renault was running parallel to the front of the van now.

Dropping his MAC, Bishop pulled himself through the window of the car, grabbed the door handle of the van's front door and jerked it open.

The driver looked surprised.

Then he looked scared.

Gripping the steering wheel to maintain control, he swung his left leg out to kick Bishop away. The Canadian swerved, dangling between the Renault and the van. He threw himself forward and grabbed the man's neck and collar.

The IRA driver let go of the steering wheel and fought back, trying desperately to push Bishop away. The van went out of control, veering to the right. It smashed out the Renault's front fender and almost forced it off the road. Abruptly the steering wheel jerked right, sending the van toward the ditch.

Bishop and the Irish Provo scrambled for control in the cramped confines of the front seat. The IRA attacker grabbed Bishop. The Canadian forced his hand against his face in an attempt to push him away from the wheel. He felt teeth sinking into his palm.

He swung his right arm back and slugged hard, connecting at the driver's temple. From the corner of his eyes he saw the grassy ditch and a low stone wall coming up fast.

The van hit. The world became an upside-down blur as the roll battered the two embattled opponents back and forth.

LIAM O'TOOLE LAY IN DARKNESS, sometimes feeling more dead than alive. He dreamed often of Susy. The dreams were troubled, anxious. He followed her through the corridors of an old castle, out a doorway into a tiny garden and then through the tiny rooms of the shabby house he had lived in as a boy. Sometimes she looked back. But she never stopped, and he was never able to catch up with her.

Once, through his closed eyes, he sensed a light in the cold cellar prison. He opened them. She was standing there in the center of the room, bathed in a golden glow. He reached out to her. His breath caught in his throat and she faded with a smile, only to be replaced by the cruel laughing face of Seamus Killerbey.

O'Toole was tormented by pain. Killerbey's bullet had ripped through the center of his hand like a crucifixion nail, blowing skin and bone out the other side. They had beaten him before they took him back to the cellar of the old stone farmhouse, and they had wrapped the hand in a dirty rag to stop the bleeding.

He didn't know how long he had been left there on the cold stone floor, in complete darkness, without food or water. A man can drink his own urine seven times. He'd remembered that from his survival training in the Army.

The urine kept him alive a little longer.

He knew the end was going to come sooner or later, though. If Seamus Killerbey and his goons didn't get him, the gangrene that had begun to rot his hand would. He felt as if he were burning alive, yet his hand touched cold stone walls. It was the fever. He had lost all sensation in the other hand.

He thought a lot about dying; now he knew it as a certainty. Sometimes he raged against it; other times he was frightened. But lately, in the timeless darkness that measured out his last hours, he felt strangely peaceful. He thought of Susy in America. When he was dead, she would be safe.

He knew they would come for him sooner or later, but when they did, it surprised him.

The door swung open, and a square of blinding white light burst in upon the room. O'Toole squeezed his eyes tightly shut against the pain and shielded his face with his one good hand.

There was no mistaking the source of the laughter. It was Seamus Killerbey, the Devil himself. "It warms my heart to see Liam O'Toole reduced to this." He cackled again.

"All right, lads. Take him upstairs and clean him up. I want him looking good for his last ride."

O'Toole was lifted bodily to his feet, a man on each side, and dragged through the door and up the stairs. He was given a towel and a basin of hot water in a room upstairs. Clean clothes lay on a chair. Danny and Rion watched him malevolently, their guns aimed and cocked. This time there would be no mistakes.

Gradually O'Toole's eyes adjusted to the light. It was morning. Outside, the blue sky lay glorious over the green hills of the Emerald Isle. When he was finished, a plate of food was brought to him, and he poked at it, his appetite gone. Still, he felt some of his energy returning. And with it, sensation in his hand. It burned with pain.

After a while, Seamus Killerbey called for the prisoner to be brought out.

He was taken into the large central room downstairs, which was furnished with only a long wooden table and a dozen old chairs. They sat him in one of them and tied his arms to the back of it.

Killerbey ordered the other men from the room.

"Is your hand hurting you now?" Seamus sneered when they were alone. "Well, don't worry your head about it. You won't be needing it. The military tribunal of the Irish Republican Army has tried you in camera. You were convicted. The sentence is death."

"Some trial," O'Toole said in a low voice.

Killerbey pursed his lips. "We did away with a few of the formalities for the sake of expediency. You had your chance, Liam. But you tried to escape, and before that you wired the remote on the milk truck so it wouldn't work. I discovered the mistake in time. The operation was a complete success. Sixty-four dead and twice as many wounded. Some horribly. Some forever."

"And Susy. What have you done with her?"

Killerbey paused before answering. Finally he smiled generously at the prisoner.

"We've decided to leave her be, you'll be glad to know. After all, we still have you. And you're going to die. Yes, there'll be joy in Ireland for our people when they know that the stool pigeon who betrayed Thomas Murphy has finally met justice."

"I didn't betray the man." O'Toole shook his head slowly. "I woke up to what he was doing, and I didn't like it. But I never betrayed him."

"Are you suggesting there might be a better betrayer now, Liam? And that he might still be among us?" Killerbey leaned over the table so his taunting face was close to O'Toole's. "Well, you know, you could be right. Not that it matters now, does it?"

"You don't really care who you kill, do you, Seamus? As long as someone pays for it and you get the credit."

"That's right, Liam! This will make me a legend among the people, as popular as Thomas Murphy himself. I'll be leader of the provisional wing of the IRA for all of Ireland. But let me tell you something." Killerbey's voice was thin and deadly. "The betrayal of Thomas Murphy—by whomever—was nothing compared to the betrayal that put you in our hands. Nothing!"

He roared the last word, then nodded, his eyes aflame with delight. O'Toole looked at him, trying to make sense of what the man was saying. Killerbey's voice sank to a mere whisper.

"Yes, Liam. You, too, were betrayed."

The door opened and Rion stuck his head into the room. Killerbey looked up.

"The Father's here, Seamus. He's got someone with him. Says he's on the lam, a fugitive from the constabulary."

Barely had the man finished speaking than the door was pushed open farther. Darby O'Goole marched briskly into the room. The tall priest glanced quickly at O'Toole before turning to Killerbey.

"You understand fully the implications of what I told you on the telephone," he said guardedly. "These people must be stopped."

"It's not a problem, Father," the IRA leader said smoothly. "I've just sent six men out to take care of them. And besides, we're ready to move with the project. Who's this you got with you?" He looked over the priest's shoulder at the man who had followed him into the room. It was Simon McVaghey.

"A fugitive from East Belfast. He was hiding ammunition in his house when the RUC came calling. He has to go underground."

"And you brought him here?" Killerbey said with astonishment.

"It won't make any difference. This place is too risky. We've been using it too long, anyway. And after the latest offensive, the police will be everywhere. There are better places to hide. More comfortable places, for that matter, Seamus."

"True." He looked at O'Toole. "Like the place we got this traitor from." He turned to the fugitive.

"You there. What's your name?"

McVaghey told him.

"Who'd you work for in Belfast, then?"

Carefully Simon McVaghey recited the answers the police had made him memorize.

Killerbey nodded with approval. "We'll have to move you somewhere else. As the Father says, it's best we close this place down. And we've got to do it right away. You know the Dublin-Belfast train, do you?"

McVaghey nodded.

"This afternoon we're going to send that train straight into the heart of Belfast at full speed. With no driver and no brakes. And this traitor here, Liam O'Toole, strapped to the front of the engine as it slams into the rush-hour crowd at the Victoria Street Station." Killerbey leaned his head back and laughed uproariously.

THE WHITE VAN TEETERED on its side on top of the stone wall that bordered the field next to the highway. It decided to go over. Bishop landed upside down, but on top of the struggling driver. He forced the man's arm behind his back in a half nelson. He heard Nanos's voice. The Greek sounded worried.

"Hey, Geoff. Geoff, you all right?" The Greek's face appeared at the window on the passenger's side.

"Yeah, I'm fine. Get this guy out of here first."

With some difficulty, Nanos got the battered door opened. He shoved the stubby barrel of his MAC into the man's nape. "No funny stuff," he warned as the man crawled from the wreckage. Bishop pulled himself out. He felt bruised all over. As though he'd just been in a car accident.

Nanos had the IRA man on his knees, and was pulling his head back and stabbing the MAC into the underside of his chin.

"We want to know where Liam O'Toole is."

"Never heard of him."

"Well, maybe you heard of a 30-round mag of highspeed lead smashing your skull to shit."

"You'll get nothing out of me," the man said bravely.

Nanos jerked the man to his feet, possessed by a fury Bishop had never seen before.

"I'll get it out of you, you fucking bastard. Liam O'Toole's my friend! I'll get it out of your murderous ass." He pushed the man forward roughly, the MAC still leveled up against his neck, and marched him onto the road where the Renault was parked.

"On the ground!" Nanos screamed.

The prisoner flattened himself on the road face-down. Nanos put his foot on the man's head and ground it into the gravel. With his free hand he lifted the hood of the car.

"You tell us where Liam O'Toole is!" he screamed at the prisoner. The man remained silent. Nanos reached down, grabbed him by the collar and jerked him to his feet. He threw him against the front fender of the car and forced his head down over the hot engine block. Bishop watched, tight-lipped.

"Now you gonna tell us where we can find our friend?"

The prisoner was gasping with fear. He felt the heat from the car engine bombarding his face. He shook his head quickly.

Nanos pushed the man's face against the side of the engine. The IRA prisoner screamed, his legs flying into the air as the skin burned off his face. The Greek held him there. The smell of burning flesh and the cries of pain were awesome.

"You gonna tell us!" Nanos shouted in his rage. "Tell us!"

The Irishman writhed, his screams coming in short chilling gasps. "Ya, ya, please, stop...I..."

Nanos pulled the man's head up. The side of his tormented race was raw red. His knees collapsed beneath him and he fell dully against the fender, sobbing and gasping for air.

"At the stone farmhouse. Ten kilometers straight down the road. He's a prisoner there."

"Who else is there?" The man hesitated, and Nanos jerked him up and got ready for a repeat performance.

"No, noo!" the prisoner screamed as the engine block came around for the second time. "Six men! With Seamus Killerbey!"

Nanos relaxed. He pulled the man from under the hood and let him drop on the road beside the car.

The Toyota van carrying the other mercs pulled abreast of them just as he finished. Barrabas, Hatton, Beck and Starfoot got out. They looked at the prisoner. The open hood on the car told the tale. The mercs were silent.

"Liam's at a farmhouse ten kliks down the road. There are six IRA men there. The leader's name is Seamus Killerbey." Nanos spoke in a low, quiet voice, the explosive rage of a moment earlier drained from him.

There was a brief silence. Hatton spoke first.

"I'll get the first-aid kit." She looked at the IRA prisoner and headed for the Toyota.

The man was weeping now. "They'll kill me," he sobbed. He looked at the mercs standing around him. "Please. Kill me first. Don't let them do it. When they find out I've told you they'll . . ." His voice thinned to a high-pitched, hysterical whine.

Barrabas turned away and looked at Nanos and Bishop.

"That was some mighty good work from both of you. You make a good team." He didn't care if the two mercs didn't like each other, but if they were going to work together, they had to have mutual respect. One way or another, he was determined to make them earn it.

Both men looked slightly embarrassed.

"Hey, some bullet holes," Nanos said, shrugging off Barrabas's statement and looking at the back of the Toyota. The Renault was a mess, too. "The car rental agency's going to love us."

Without warning, their prisoner jumped to his feet, his eyes wild. He rushed the Greek, grabbing his submachine gun. Nanos pulled back as the man's hands pressed down on his fingers. The MAC fired.

The Irishman's gut took a solid payload of lead. He stopped struggling. He looked at Alex, his eyes big and surprised. Without a word, he sank slowly to his knees and collapsed, face first, in the gravel.

"Shit." Nanos was almost in shock. The man was dead by the time the mercs saw it happen. Lee Hatton had just come around the van with her black medical case. She stopped and looked at the body.

"I didn't want to kill the guy," Nanos said in disbelief.

"Ten kilometers down this road?" Barrabas asked him.

"That's what the guy said."

Barrabas scratched the side of his head with the barrel of his MAC-10. "Six of them, six of us."

"They've got a hostage," Bishop pointed out.

Barrabas nodded.

"We'll drive—then walk the last klik. We can split up and come in on three sides." He pulled one of his long thin cigars from his breast pocket. It was a little crushed from the slide across the restaurant parking lot. He peeled the wrapper off, stuck it in his mouth and jerked his head toward the Toyota. "Let's go."

14

The cavalcade of IRA vehicles was lined up in front of the farmhouse when O'Toole was pushed outside. The priest's big black car was to one side. Behind it, a dark-blue Volkswagen van idled. Three of the IRA men sat astride motorcycles. O'Toole looked quickly for the red Norton. Anyone riding it would be blown to pieces with the volatile bombards he had doctored before his escape. Killerbey intimated that he alone rode the bike. Obviously he didn't ride it often enough.

As O'Toole was pushed forward toward the back of the van he saw it. The Norton had been wheeled inside and strapped alongside two other bikes. O'Toole was made to sit on the floor beside it. His arms and feet were bound with tight cord, and a hood was pulled over his face.

Killerbey walked with Father O'Goole to the priest's car, with Simon McVaghey following.

"Take him to the safe house in Belfast. The one on Newtownards Road. It's so close to military intelllligence headquarters they'll never think to comb the area. They're too busy digging themselves out of the ruins we left them yesterday.''

"And where will you be intercepting the train?"

"At Lingan. We'll board at the station there. It's thirty kilometers out of Belfast. The other lads will take over the switching station and force them to switch the freight train onto the passenger line. Rion, Danny and I'll get rid of the engineer just after Lisburn. We'll hop off then and the boys will be meeting us with the van. We'll make our getaway on the motorbikes. They're faster, and they can go anywhere.''

"May God be with you," the priest said, giving his blessing.

Seamus smiled. "He already is!"

For a moment, the priest thought that Killerbey was referring to himself.

Quickly the men mounted their vehicles, and the convoy left the farm, turning east and driving in the direction of Belfast.

LEE HATTON COUNTED DOWN the kilometers as the Toyota van sped along the gravel road. Alex and Bishop followed in the battered Renault. For some distance, green fields on either side of them climbed toward the bright-blue horizon. At the eight-klik point, the land suddenly fell away to a wide shallow valley. Two kilometers farther, they could see the stone farmhouse and adjoining barn, set back from the road. There was no sign of life. Barrabas searched in vain for some kind of cover to launch their attack from.

"Looks like we're going to have to walk right up and say hello," Billy Two commented from the back seat.

"Lee, slow down," Barrabas ordered. He leaned out his window and waved the Renault forward until it was driving parallel to him. Alex rolled his window down to hear the Colonel.

"Drive ahead of us about a klik past the farm, and come in on foot from that side. Use the ditch for cover."

Nanos waved to acknowledge the instructions, and the Renault roared ahead of them.

Barrabas rolled up the window and turned to Billy Two and Nate Beck. "I want you two to slip out the back of the van and make it to the farmhouse on foot from this side. Double-time. Stay in the ditch. It's not deep, but the stone wall running on the other side gives you another three feet, so you should make it most of the way unseen. Lee and I are going to have a bit of engine trouble just outside the farmhouse. We'll give you time to get take up positions before we go in."

"How much time?" Nate asked, glancing at his watch.

"I have exactly a quarter to one," Barrabas said. "Ten minutes."

The mercs set their watches. Billy Two opened the back door of the van as Lee slowed their speed to twenty kilometers an hour. Beck dropped out first, landing in a crouch on the road and slithering quickly across the gravel into the ditch. Billy Two followed. The shallow drainage bed came waist high on the two men, but Barrabas was right. The low stone wall along the fields on the other side obscured the farmhouse—and the SOBs, if anyone was watching from the farmhouse.

Lee maintained a low speed, taking her time until they were almost at the driveway of the farm. She shoved the gearshift into first and started pumping the clutch. The van reared and bucked, lurching and sliding on the slippery gravel. The gears shrieked and died in a fading whine as the van stalled. She floored the accelerator, flooding the engine. Then she tried to start the car up. The ignition ground away, turning the engine, but the flooded carburetor prevented it from catching.

"You wanted car trouble. Think that'll convince them?"

Barrabas smiled. "We'll find out. I hope the gas will drain from the carburetor by the time we're ready to leave."

Lee shrugged. "It'll just take a couple of minutes."

"Like I said..."

Lee held up both hands with her fingers crossed. "Let's just call this 'added incentive.'" She turned the key again in a mock attempt to start the van.

"Guess I'll just go out, have a look under the hood and play the perplexed Yankee tourist."

Barrabas tucked his MAC under his jacket and left the van. He walked toward the front, quickly eyeing the farmhouse a hundred meters away. There was no sign of life, and the windows were dark. That didn't mean no one was inside, watching. He leaned over the engine and studied it carefully, continuing his sideways glances at the farmhouse.

He went around and climbed back into the van.

"Will it start now?"

"Should," said Lee. "If I floor it."

She pushed down the accelerator and turned the ignition. The engine roared to life.

"Drive into the farmyard as close to the front doors as possible and keep riding the clutch to make the van look sick."

Lee did as instructed. The van leaped and jerked up the driveway until they were only a few meters from the front doors.

"Look at the ground," Barrabas told her.

It was tracked with footprints and tire prints.

"I get the feeling they've pulled out." He reached into his pocket and tore out the lining. He fitted his hand through the hole and grasped the trigger of the concealed MAC-10. Then he opened the door. "Only one way to find out." He stepped from the van with a last survey of the windows and the outbuildings. Still no sign of life.

His watch said five to one.

His body tensed for action, he walked carefully to the front door and knocked with his free hand.

No answer.

He knocked again. He waited a moment, looking around and casually meeting Lee's eyes. With a flicker of his eyes he signaled her to get ready. She opened the van door. Barrabas turned to face the farmhouse again. Like lightning, his foot came up and smashed into the wood near the handle.

The door splintered and whirled inward.

Barrabas spun himself sideways against the doorframe, the MAC-10 protruding from his jacket and pointing in.

He was met with silence.

Lee stood behind the car door, a MAC resting on the top hinge and aimed into the house.

Barrabas crouched and whipped across the open doorway, throwing a burst of fire inside. He ran through.

Lee fanned in behind him, and they stood back to back, the death-spitting ends of their SMGs circling the room.

It was empty.

They heard a crash and the splinter of wood at the back of the house. A mean voice shouted, "Awright, fuckers. It's Alex the Greek and I've come to get you!"

Barrabas motioned Lee toward a doorway on one side of the room. He went into the room ahead of him, where a long wooden table sat among a dozen empty chairs. He spotted a dark stain on the side of one of them. He touched it and looked at his fingers. It was blood.

Nanos burst in from the other doorway, his eyes wild. He saw Barrabas. The Colonel heard Bishop's footsteps thudding up a stairway somewhere in the house.

"Nothing, sir!" Nanos looked shocked.

"Search the place from top to bottom."

Barrabas turned and ran out of the farmhouse. Just as he moved out of the front door, he saw Starfoot and Beck jumping over the low stone field wall and racing toward the barn.

Beck headed for the side door, which was secured by a padlock.

"Stop!" Barrabas shouted.

About to crash down on the lock, Beck froze, his MAC in midair.

Billy Two threw himself forward in a running tackle, hurtling into the surprised merc. The two men flew backward away from the barn, with Billy Two hanging on to Beck as they rolled on the dusty ground.

They had barely landed, when the barn blew with a mighty roar, instantaneously transformed into a roaring inferno by the explosion.

DARBY O'GOOLE'S BIG BLACK CAR rolled to a halt by the curb in a rundown area off Newtownards Road. Tiny brick houses were sandwiched between bombed-out storefronts, and the one remaining pub had sandbags in front of the window. Darby O'Goole emerged from his car and looked quickly up and down the street.

"Let's go now—quickly," he leaned inside and told Simon McVaghey.

The simple, well-meaning man did as he was instructed, smiling stupidly.

Darby O'Goole gave the fugitive a strange look. He was beginning to feel there was something odd about this man. He didn't seem like IRA material. But he had a responsibility to look after his own—at least until he could make direct contact with McVaghey's cell to confirm his story.

"This way," he said. He strode briskly across the sidewalk and up the steps to one of the little brick houses, knocked three times, paused and knocked a fourth. The door opened and O'Goole hustled the fugitive inside.

McVaghey took one look at the woman who stood in the hallway and his mouth fell open. He knew her. She worked at the tea shop down the street from where he lived with his mum and dad.

"This is the man I told you about," O'Goole said.

"But this man is..." The woman stared at McVaghey, wide-eyed.

Suddenly Simon McVaghey knew something was terribly wrong. He bolted. Fast as he could, he turned and ran through the open door and down the street without a backward glance.

Darby O'Goole and the woman at the safe house watched speechlessly as McVaghey escaped.

"Damn!" the priest cursed. "Damn him to hell. Damn them all!"

NATE BECK AND BILLY TWO felt the heat of the burning barn sweep over them as they picked themselves up from the dirt and ran toward the farmhouse. The wooden building was quickly consumed by an immense ball of fire reaching ten meters into the sky.

"Holy shit," Beck swore as he came up to Barrabas. "How'd you know?"

"Instinct. They've pulled out. It makes sense that they'd leave a little surprise behind for whoever came looking."

"Instinct, Colonel," Billy Two said brightly. "That's what I was trying to tell you back in Wyoming."

Barrabas nodded doubtfully. "Yeah, but mine is based on tried experience, Billy. You keep talking about visions."

The Osage warrior sighed. He could never make these white men understand.

Geoff Bishop, Nanos and Lee Hatton emerged from the farmhouse.

"I found these in an upstairs room, Colonel." Bishop held a soiled shirt and trousers, stiff with dried blood and grime. "And this." He held up a dirty bandage.

Lee Hatton took it from him. Blood had soaked through the strip of cloth. "Some of the blood is fresh. Whoever wore this bandage—" Lee avoided speculating about the person's identity ''—was still bleeding an hour ago. The wound is badly infected, too. Maybe they just shot the receiver out of Liam's hand.''

''There was also a tray of food—still fairly fresh— in the room where this was,'' Bishop added.

Barrabas looked at the clothes. ''They don't feed a man and give him a fresh change of clothes when they're going to kill him right away.''

It was the most encouragement the mercs had had since they arrived in Northern Ireland.

''Is there a phone in the house?'' he asked.

''Not anymore,'' Lee said. She pointed to the telephone lines that ran past the burning barn from the road. They trailed on the ground, ripped out by the explosion.

''What now, Colonel?'' Nanos asked.

''Let's get back to Belfast.'' Barrabas said. ''And at the first telephone we see I want to talk to Major Topman again...tell him about this place and see if he's onto anything.''

O'TOOLE PRAYED THAT THE BOMBARDS with the sawed-off fuses hidden under the red Norton would blow and put an end to it all—to his ordeal and to the murderous bastards who had him prisoner. Although the van rode roughly over the country roads, he had no such luck. Sawing fuses off live mortars was a tricky business. He had been hurrying. Probably he had not cut them short enough.

The blue Volkswagen van finally stopped at the high wire fence that surrounded the freight yards at Lingan, a small town on the Dublin-to-Belfast train route.

"Gag him, lads, and take his mask off so he can see where he's walking," Killerbey ordered.

With a rag crammed into his mouth, O'Toole was dragged from the back of the van. Rion used wire cutters to slip open the perimeter fence. The men slipped through, and the van drove off.

They pushed their prisoner through the railway yard, darting between the freight cars on their sidings and running quickly across empty tracks. Finally they came to the last train. Twenty cars ahead, the engine was running.

"Watch him," Killerbey told Rion. He waved Danny after him, and they ran down the train to the caboose. The IRA leader went up the metal steps on the back platform.

The conductor and a couple of men were sitting in the tiny car, drinking tea. They looked up with surprise when they saw him at the door.

Killerbey opened it as Danny came up behind him.

The railwaymen stared down the barrels of automatic rifles.

Killerbey and Danny fired simultaneously. The bullets ripped into the victims' bodies, dancing them in deathly jigs against the walls. Their china cups shattered on the floor.

"You can always tell the bloody Protestants," Killerbey sneered. "They're the ones with the jobs."

The two men raced from the caboose back to where they'd left Rion guarding O'Toole.

"Bring him along," Killerbey ordered.

Once again O'Toole was jerked to his feet and pushed along the siding toward the head of the train. Danny crawled underneath the fuel car and grasped the ladder that led up to the engineer's compartment as Killerbey mounted on the other side.

Both men arrived in the same place at the same time. The two engineers turned from the wheel. The hijackers aimed their guns.

"On your knees, fellows, for the time being. We're sending this train to a special destination."

The two engineers raised their hands slowly and sank to the floor.

IN BELFAST, Major Topman reached across his desk to pick up the receiver. He flicked his eyes once again at the man sitting in the chair on the other side of his desk. His face reflected the disturbing news he'd just received.

"A Nile Barrabas is on the line, sir," his secretary told him. "He says it's urgent."

"Put him through."

Without pausing for formalities, Barrabas explained what happened in Kelligro and at the abandoned safe house.

"So it was you, was it, Nile? The reports just came in on that. It sounded like all hell broke loose in Armagh. Considering the carnage at that restaurant at the crossroads, I thought we were dealing with major warfare between the Ulster defence force—the Protestant terrorists—and the IRA."

"Well, the farmhouse turned out to be one big dead end," Barrabas told him. "Are there any developments at your end?"

Topman cleared his throat and looked again at the man in his office. Simon McVaghey returned his gaze with a foolish smile.

"Well, actually, Nile, there is something that might interest you. Remember the man we set up to infiltrate the IRA escape routes and safe houses? He's come back. And I think he was at the same farmhouse earlier today."

"Did he see O'Toole?"

Topman cupped his hand over the telephone and spoke to McVaghey. "These men you saw, by any chance did they have a prisoner?"

Simon McVaghey furrowed his brow and thought hard, trying to remember everything he'd seen that morning. "Uh, there was a man tied up. Do you mean that?"

Topman spluttered. "Why didn't you tell me this before, you fool!"

McVaghey looked hurt. "No one asked me," he pouted unhappily.

"What happened to him?"

McVaghey shrugged and thought harder. His face brightened. "He went with the other men. In the van with the motorcycles."

"Fool," Topman said again, under his breath. He spoke back into the telephone. "Yes, he saw your man, Nile. Still alive, apparently. At least when they left the farmhouse."

"So where's he now?" Barrabas asked.

Topman coughed. "Well, actually, Nile, I think I can help you out on that. It seems the leader of the group is this man I told you about, the informer on the Thomas Murphy case some years ago. Seamus Killerbey. And, er, well, it seems they have some kind of plan to run a driverless train straight through the heart of Belfast this afternoon. Where are you now?"

"Just a minute."

Topman heard Barrabas shouting to one of his men. He came back on the line.

"Just outside Lisburn."

Topman coughed again. "Well, according to our information, the train is heading through Lisburn right about now. We've just sent half the army— Hello? Hello, Nile?" Topman flicked the button on the telephone rapidly to restore the connection. He heard a click, followed by the droning dial tone.

15

The two engineers trembled at the controls of the giant metal machine as they drove the train toward Belfast with the barrels of guns pointed at their heads. Just after Lingan they passed the switching house, and the engine made a sudden turn onto a different set of tracks.

Seamus laughed joyfully. "Right on cue! Good work, laddies, and a tip o' the hat!" He leaned out the window and saluted toward the switching house, where his men were executing the linemen who had survived the initial attack.

He jabbed one of the engineers with his gun. "Now drive it fast until I tell you otherwise."

The train clipped along, reaching a speed of a hundred kilometers an hour.

"Hey, you." Killerbey pressed his gun into the shoulder of one of the drivers and spun him around. "How much faster will this thing do?"

The engineer shrugged. "Another twenty kilometers an hour. But it would be getting a wee bit dangerous at that speed. The freight cars are empty and top heavy. They'll begin to sway. There'd be danger of a derailment at that speed.''

Killerbey smiled. "All the better. Especially if it happens in downtown Belfast.''

Twenty minutes later, the train slowed as it headed through the town of Lisburn, thirteen kilometers out of Belfast.

"That's right, slow it right down and stop it on the other side of Lisburn.''

He watched the engineers carefully. The train had three controls he was interested in: the throttle, the brakes and the emergency hydraulics. The first two were easy. The third involved a cable running along the roof of the cab, with a long red handle suspended from it.

The houses of Lisburn dwindled as the train left the village and entered the countryside again. The Volkswagen van and three more IRA men on motorcycles were waiting at a level crossing half a kilometer ahead.

"You ready, Rion?" Killerbey shouted.

"Aye, Seamus, ready.''

"Good." Killerbey looked at O'Toole, who sat bound and gagged on the metal floor. "The traitor meets his end. But not without one last grand look at his native city. Liam O'Toole, you're going to see Belfast from a new perspective," the IRA leader gloated.

"Stop the train!" Killerbey commanded.

The engineers closed the throttle and pulled back the long brake handle. With a hissing of the steam hydraulics, the train slowly ground to a halt just before the road. Killerbey's waiting men swarmed around the engine.

"On your knees," Killerbey ordered the two engineers. "Facing the controls."

Trembling uncontrollably, the two men did as they were commanded.

Killerbey slipped a handgun from his jacket and placed it squarely in the back of the first engineer's head. He pulled the trigger. The man's brains splattered against the glass dials along the control panel as a long bloody gush followed.

Having seen a preview of his own death, the second engineer tried to run.

There was no place to go.

He turned, squeezing back against the blood-covered controls, his face contorted in a scream. Danny and Rion grabbed him. It took all their strength to combat their victim's last frantic struggles. They pulled him back to the center of the cab and forced him to kneel.

Killerbey grabbed a handful of hair to hold the man's head steady. "I like to do my executions properly," he said, putting the barrel of the gun against the man's head. He fired a single shot. The bullet passed out the engineer's right eye socket, smashing into a glass dial on the control panel. Rion and Danny let go. The man's body dropped and a thick pool of blood spread quickly over the floor.

Rion and Danny lifted O'Toole and dragged him from the cab. They threw him from the ladder. His hands still bound, he landed heavily and painfully on his side.

Killerbey looked down from the window of the engine's cab. "Did you break an arm or a leg, Liam? Aw, that's too bad. Well, don't be worrying about it." His voice became merry. "You won't be needing them much longer." He threw a coil of thick rope down to the two IRA men.

"There you go, lads. It's time for Liam O'Toole's last ride to Belfast. Tie him to the front of the train and we'll smear him on the bricks of Victoria Station."

The echo of Seamus Killerbey's mirth followed Liam O'Toole as he was dragged forward. They tied him, spread-eagle, over the giant headlight of the diesel engine.

BARRABAS AND STARFOOT took over the Renault and drove out of Lisburn with the speedometer climbing steadily to past a hundred and forty kilometers an hour. Cars swerved out of their way and pedestrians ran for their lives as the two tore through the normally quiet streets of the town. The other mercs followed in the Toyota van. The distance between the two vehicles grew as Starfoot floored the Renault.

On the outskirts of Lisburn, the road turned and ran parallel to the railroad tracks. The train was tiny in the distance, but they saw the train. It was stopped at a level crossing in the middle of some fields, half a klick off the main highway.

"They're making their run for it," Barrabas snarled, his teeth clenched. They saw the van and the motorcycles on the other side of the crossing. IRA men milled around. Another man was scrambling down from the engine's cab.

They came to the crossroad. The Renault's tires screamed with Starfoot's sharp left turn. The level crossing was straight ahead.

"My God," Barrabas swore. "It's him."

Liam O'Toole was spread-eagled across the front of the train.

The IRA men saw the car heading toward them just as the train started to move. It inched toward the level crossing, then began picking up speed. Two of the IRA men raised their rifles. One of them was aiming at the Renault. The other had his sight set on Liam O'Toole. The train surged forward.

Barrabas leaned out the car window and sent a spray of bullets from the MAC in their direction. The little automatic rifle jarred painfully in his hand as he struggled to keep his grip on it. From that distance, accuracy with a MAC-10 is worse than nil. But the weapon did the trick.

The IRA men scrambled for their motorcycles. Barrabas emptied the mag at the escaping men. Accuracy was improving as the gap between the Renault and the crossing closed. One man flew back off the seat of his bike and lay in the dirt. A second skidded as he turned, flying sideways as his motorcycle went out of control.

Barrabas pulled himself back inside and jammed in a fresh mag.

"Head down, Colonel!" Billy Two shouted.

Both men ducked under the dash. Billy Two held the steering wheel steady and drove blind. The windshield kicked in as a rain of lead showered them with glass diamonds.

When it was over, Barrabas came up and stuck his MAC arm out the window again. The train was almost at the level crossing, and its speed was increasing. So far, none of the IRA men had hit O'Toole.

The Colonel squeezed the trigger and emptied the full mag in a steady burst as the enemy tried to get their motorbikes turned to get out of there. Another one skidded and fell sideways. The train reached the edge of the crossing just as Barrabas's mag emptied. There were no stray bullets. Lead chunked into metal. A gas tank blew. The rider burned in a ball of flame that seared him from crotch to head. His screams were high-pitched and short.

The train pulled across the road.

Starfoot braked and the Renault screeched in a long slide, halting inches away from the passing engine. The two mercs ran from the car. Barrabas got there first.

As the cab passed, he grabbed the metal ladder, almost jerking his arms from his sockets. Billy Two ran alongside and also grabbed hold.

The two men scrambled up the ladder and pulled themselves through the open door.

The scene was gruesome. The floor of the cab swirled in blood that lapped over the toes of their boots. The bodies of the two engineers lay in a heap below the brain-splattered control panel.

"It's been shot up bad, Billy," Barrabas shouted, surveying quickly the mass of broken dials and instruments. The throttle had been ripped off, the brake handle was dismantled and the emergency brake pull hung loosely from its severed cord. "Try to stop this thing!"

Billy looked stunned.

"Stop it? How the fuck am I supposed to stop it? I don't know a fucking thing about trains!"

"Use your instincts!" the Colonel shouted. He grabbed the long metal handle that had been torn from the brakes and smashed the front windows of the cab. Starfoot boosted him up as Barrabas crawled through, ripping his clothes and his skin on the deadly shards of glass.

He came up slowly outside, feet apart, and began moving forward on top of the engine.

The train had gathered speed quickly and was beginning its last hurtle toward Belfast.

Billy looked around the cab, trying to figure out what to do.

"Instincts, humph," he said out loud. "The white man thinks I make miracles. Heap big medicine needed here, for Christ's sake."

Then he had a feeling. It came straight from his gut.

He saw a lever halfway down the wall near the window on the right side of the cab. It was the kill switch. He didn't know how he knew it, but he did. He grabbed it and jerked it back.

Immediately the humming reverberating through the great metal beast stopped. He heard the faint whine of the dying engines. He looked at the switch. It worked. He couldn't believe it.

Turning off the engines was only half of it. The train had already reached a speed of almost a hundred kilometers an hour. Unless he found a way of braking it, they'd be halfway across Belfast before it stopped.

He looked at the ruined brakes. The guts had been torn out of the controls, and it looked like a four-hour job just to pick up all the screws and widgets. He turned around and examined the broken end of the emergency-brake cord, hanging from the ceiling. Without the leverage of the severed handle there was no way a man could pull the hydraulics open.

Somewhere in his Osage head, a smooth voice said, "Try it."

"Not you again?" Billy Two said out loud to the empty cab as the train hurtled swiftly forward on its metaled rails.

"Sure. Try it," the voice said.

Billy Two looked at the wire cord hanging loosely from the ceiling. He looked out the window and saw the Irish countryside flying past. He looked at the cord again. The white men were right. He was crazy.

"Okay," he said. "Why not?"

He spat once into the palm of each hand and rubbed them quickly together.

THE MERCS NARROWLY AVOIDED an oncoming convoy of British army jeeps and trucks as Hatton drove the Toyota van off the highway. At the level crossing, their progress was blocked by the runaway train. The military vehicles braked behind them and soldiers jumped out.

The SOBs beat them to it.

The train cut them off from the escaping IRA gang. It didn't stop them. Hatton, Nanos, Bishop and Beck leaped from the van and ran to the side of the tracks, flattening themselves on the siding. The train was going slowly enough to shoot underneath it.

Two of the escaping IRA men were out of action. One lay dead on his back; the other one was smoldering like a bonfire beside his burning bike. Two more were trying to lift their heavy motorcycles up. The last two were making their escape good. The red Norton was in the lead.

Nanos unleashed a short burst across the tracks.

An escaping IRA man saw his kneecap explode. He fell, his quarter-ton bike landing on top of him, pinning him to the ground.

The other mercs let rip. MAC fire chattered in short bursts between the wheels of the train. The second man yelped as bullets pinged into his motorcycle. He dropped the bike and started to run.

The caboose rolled by, and Hatton ran for the van to chase after the escaping man. As Lee drove up, Bishop jumped up and sprinted the fifty meters to bring down the IRA man.

Nanos and Beck arrived, breathless, with a dozen British soldiers right behind them.

"Leave those people alone!" a proper English voice commanded. "They're on our side!" An army jeep sped over the crossing, with Major Topman standing in back, shouting orders.

A blustering sergeant with a thick red mustache ran ahead of his soldiers. "Right now. We're in charge here," he shouted at the mercs.

Bishop grabbed the prisoner and forced him to his feet. The man hunched his shoulders in fear and raised his hands as the soldiers circled.

The IRA man started to back away, but there was no place to go. He was surrounded. Another group of soldiers ran toward the man pinned under the motorcycle.

The jeep pulled to a halt in front of the mercs, and Major Topman jumped down.

"Good work! Jolly good work!"

"Two of them got away on their motorcycles," Bishop told him.

"No problem, old chap. We have roadblocks set up over the entire six counties. They won't get far. Now where's Colonel Barrabas?"

The two IRA prisoners screamed for mercy as the soldiers began beating them. The four SOBs looked away; their distaste for that kind of rough justice was obvious to the Major.

"Er, yes, well. The men get a little carried away, perhaps, but it's good for morale."

"Last I saw the Colonel, he and Starfoot were climbing aboard the engine," Lee said. She pointed to the runaway train, which was growing smaller on the horizon.

"We've got to stop it!" Topman shouted. "There's another crossing five kilometers toward Belfast."

The mercs looked at one another.

"We'll meet you there," Lee said to the Major.

Topman ran for his jeep.

BARRABAS HUNCHED OVER to keep his center of gravity low, and walked forward along the top of the speeding engine with his legs wide. When he got to the front, he flattened himself on his stomach and looked down over the side.

O'Toole's face was twisted in pain, and the veins stood out along his muscled arms as he strained against the bonds that held him.

"Liam!" Barrabas shouted over the noise of the engine.

O'Toole heard his name called, and stopped his struggles for a second.

"Liam! Up here!"

O'Toole stretched his head back and looked up. He saw the Colonel's face looking down at him from the top of the engine. I'm dead...I've gone to Avalon, the bound warrior thought, naming the paradise of ancient Irish lore.

Barrabas twisted around and lowered himself on metal protrusions from the engine until he was level with O'Toole. There was a narrow bumper below the light to stand on. "Good to see you, Liam!" he shouted against the rush of the wind and the engine.

O'Toole just looked at him, speechless.

Barrabas held on to the train with one hand and pulled out a knife. He hacked swiftly at his friend's bonds, freeing one of his legs.

He heard O'Toole mutter something, and turned his head to look up the tracks. Far away, but coming at an enormous speed, was the growing headlight of another train engine.

"Shit," he whispered.

He moved across O'Toole's body and hacked faster at the rope that tied the other leg. Done. He looked behind him. The locomotive was coming at them fast, its whistle shrieking wildly to warn the driverless train.

Barrabas moved up to O'Toole's left arm and sawed at the rope where it held his bloody, infected hand.

"You okay?" Barrabas spoke sideways to O'Toole as he cut.

"Yeah." It was all O'Toole could say. It had to be a bad mad dream. Wake-up time couldn't come too soon.

Barrabas edged sideways, across O'Toole's body, and cut at the final bond. He glanced at the man's face. His eyes were almost blank. He was in shock.

"Liam."

O'Toole looked at him, baffled.

"Can you climb up over the top?"

O'Toole just stared at the Colonel. The silence meant no. Barrabas glanced over his shoulder. The oncoming train was close. Between them lay only half a kilometer of field divided by another road. He could see a convoy of army jeeps raising dust as they headed for the crossing. The brakes on the train coming toward them shrieked as the engineer tried desperately to stop.

He pushed O'Toole gently but quickly to turn him around on the narrow bumper, holding precariously to an iron handle beside the headlight. Then he grabbed the man's arms and draped them over his shoulders and around his neck. He felt O'Toole's grip tightening.

"I got it, Colonel," O'Toole said suddenly. He was coming around.

"Hang on."

Barrabas looked over his shoulder. The other train was coming fast and strong. It was big and black, its headlight a glaring cyclops eye. The whistle screamed. Barrabas started climbing up the front of the engine, straining with O'Toole on his back. There was no way the other train was going to miss them.

THE RED NORTON WAS VERY FAST and very smooth. Seamus Killerbey was soon out of sight of the runaway train. There was only one member of the gang

left, following close behind on another bike. Killerbey flagged him over and pulled to the side of the
road.

He lifted the visor on his helmet.

"Ho, Danny boy! There's another road that crosses
the track a few kilometers down. I'm going back."

"You're crazy, Seamus! The bastards just got Rion,
Davy and the others," Danny cried.

"Somehow they caught on to us, Danny. They may
be able to stop the train. I'm going to make sure Liam
O'Toole gets it. Right between the eyes. With this."
He brandished his weapon.

"And what if they're waiting for us?"

"These'll get us away." He motioned to the motorcycles they sat astride. "They go faster and they go
anywhere. Are you coming or not?"

The two men sped off, racing toward the turnoff to
the next crossing. The way led into a narrow deep valley with a wooden bridge over a small stream at the
bottom. The train tracks were on the other side of the
hill and the road led straight up. They wouldn't see the
train until they reached the top of the incline. And no
one could see them.

If O'Toole's friends had made it first, by the time
they knew what was happening it would be too late.

BARRABAS STRAINED as he climbed the front of the
train. He was pulling for two. Slowly but surely he
went higher, until he came to the top. This was the
hard part. Getting on top of the engine with O'Toole

on his back might give them a chance. Otherwise they were between a rock and a hard place, and what would be left of them the morticians could just spray off with a garden hose.

The oncoming train's whistle and the sound of its screeching brakes pounded against his eardrums as the train came closer. He put his foot on top of the enormous headlight and pushed Liam O'Toole upward, marshaling his last reserves of strength. He got him over. Then he grabbed the side of the engine and scrambled up.

He lay on the top of the engine, gasping for breath, with one hand around O'Toole to make sure the man didn't slide off. Suddenly he felt a ripple through the metal skin covering the engine.

Billy Two had done it! The runaway train was jarring to a sudden halt.

But physics has its laws. He and Liam O'Toole kept going. And there was nothing to grab on to.

He clutched desperately at O'Toole as they slid back along the surface. The train's hydraulic brakes began a spine-shattering screech.

"Hang on!" he shouted as they went over the front of the train. He grabbed O'Toole around the neck and under his arm. There was the iron handle beside the headlight. Barrabas reached out. He grabbed.

He got it.

He forced O'Toole against the front of the train, pushing against velocity. The shrieks from both trains were deafening. A hot metallic smell filled the air as the metal wheels ground against the brakes.

The train stopped.

A sudden release of tension told him the ordeal was over. He relaxed his grip. O'Toole heaved a sigh. Barrabas started laughing in amazement. The two trains were within kissing distance of each other. The big headlights stared across the narrow road at the level crossing as the British army poured across the highway. The Toyota van was out in front, and Major Topman stood, brave and erect, in the back of an open jeep.

Arms rose up to meet Barrabas and O'Toole as they climbed down from the front of the engine, and the other mercs burst through the crowd. Lee ran to Liam O'Toole and threw her arms around him in a big hug. Nanos looked as if he were going to smile himself in half. Barrabas strode away from the crowd just as Billy Two jogged around the engine.

"You stopped it," the Colonel said, still laughing from the adrenaline hangover. "How'd you do it?" He noticed deep, red burn lines across the Indian's palms.

Billy smiled mysteriously. "You wouldn't understand."

There was a ruckus as Major Topman burst through the crowd that had gathered. A coterie of journalists followed, with photographers snapping soldiers and trains from every angle. The major had alerted the media.

"Who stopped it? Who stopped the train?" one of them babbled as he ran by.

"That one there...with the red hair," Barrabas said, pointing. "Liam O'Toole. He's Ireland's hero today."

Suddenly mobbed, and still nearly in shock, O'Toole pushed away from them. He walked with Hatton and Starfoot toward the Colonel.

The sound of motorcycles coming over the hill from the other direction made Barrabas turn. Two riders burst over the crest. He saw orange muzzle fire flashing. The mercs dived for cover as the first line of British soldiers went down on their knees and raised their rifles.

A line of assault fire mowed through the two motorcyclists.

Killerbey had counted on surprise.

He hadn't expected the army.

Danny took a bullet in his leg and flew back, loosing control of his bike. It drove out from under him and skidded sideways down the road, its engine screaming.

The game was up for Seamus Killerbey. The bullets missed him, but he had time enough to see Liam O'Toole alive and well. He whipped the Norton around, hugging the ground in a tight circle.

The Red Devil does it again, he thought. The bike easily made the sharp turn. It was the smoothest thing on two wheels.

He turned the throttle fully and the bike soared away from the riflemen at the train. Danny lay sprawled on his back on the road, his leg useless. He looked up just in time to see the red devil coming straight at him. His eyes bulged and his mouth opened for a scream.

Killerbey saw him. He might have turned, but he was in a hurry.

The bike ran straight up the middle of the wounded man, crushing him into the road and choking the scream before it began. The motorbike thumped up, left the ground and came down with a thud.

The bombards blew.

Barrabas and O'Toole saw the last of Seamus Killerbey sprayed into the sky with other bits of red junk.

"How in hell did that happen?" Barrabas said with amazement.

"God loves Ireland," answered O'Toole.

A white projectile flew toward them, hit the ground, bounced and landed at O'Toole's feet.

It was Seamus Killerbey's head, still inside the helmet. A trickle of blood ran from the nose, curving around the lips, which had been frozen into a crazy smile.

"You know this guy?" the Colonel asked O'Toole.

"Everyone knows the Devil."

Major Topman strode briskly forward from the line of soldiers. "Well done, I say. Well done, old boys!" he chirped. He looked at Killerbey's lower half, hanging upside down in the branches of a tree. A string of intestines hung like macabre sausages.

"I always said Seamus Killerbey didn't have any guts," the Major commented. "I was wrong."

Barrabas looked at O'Toole. The man was thin and white. His hand was a mess. "You look like hell," he said.

"I feel like—" O'Toole's eyes rolled upward and his knees buckled. Barrabas caught him before he hit the ground.

16

Liam O'Toole opened his eyes. Where am I? he thought. The room was painted blue, with white trimming. The wide window to his left revealed the spring buds of some trees and a deep-blue sky. He was in a bed with clean white sheets and heaped with blankets.

His mind raced, piecing together the events of the previous week of his life. It was too crazy. It must have been a dream. But he looked at his left hand. It was swathed in bandages and looked like a white boxing glove. Then he saw the clear plastic tube running from his arm up to a plastic bag suspended from a chrome stand. Clear liquid dripped slowly down the tube.

It was no dream.

The door opened and Lee Hatton stepped into the room. She brightened when she saw him looking at her.

"Welcome back!" she said.

"Where am I?"

"In a country house just outside Belfast. It belongs to British military intelligence. The Colonel got it through his friend, Major Topman. How're you feeling?''

"Okay. Hungry."

Lee laughed. "That's a sure sign of recovery. Know how long you've been out?''

O'Toole shook his head.

"Three days. You almost lost your hand. The best surgeon in Ireland cleaned it out and stitched it back together. Since then we've been running intravenous antibiotics through you to fight the infection. Here.''

She withdrew a thermometer from her breast pocket and stuck it in his mouth. "Keep it shut until I get back.''

She returned a few minutes later, bearing a breakfast tray. Barrabas was with her.

"Good to see you alive and recovering, Liam,'' he said warmly.

Lee took the thermometer from his mouth. "Back to normal! You can talk now, Liam.''

O'Toole looked at Barrabas, who sat on the side of the bed.

"My call got through, I guess.''

"In a way," Barrabas said. "We chased all over Northern Ireland looking for you.''

O'Toole turned his head sideways and looked out at the beautiful spring morning, as Lee set the breakfast tray in front of him.

"Is there a telephone here?'' he asked.

"Sure is," Barrabas said.

"I want to call Susy.''

Hatton and the Colonel exchanged silent glances.

"Where is she, Liam?"

"In New Jersey. They let me talk to her once. They sent her back there, but told me if I didn't get her, they'd have one of their American partisans..." His voice faded as some of the terrible memories returned. "She sounded all right, though. That was...a week ago."

"Eat first," Barrabas said. "If you're feeling well enough I want to take you for a drive to see someone special."

O'Toole's eyes brightened. "Aye, Colonel." He beamed and slipped into his native brogue. "If it's my wife you're taking me to, I'm well enough to go now."

"Eat first." This time Dr. Hatton gave the order.

AN HOUR LATER, O'Toole slipped slowly into the passenger seat of a car, with Barrabas at the wheel.

"I'm still a wee bit light-headed, I have to admit," he said as he closed the car door. The first time he stood up from the bed he'd almost passed out. But every minute he felt more of his strength returning.

Barrabas drove down the long driveway that led through the high stone walls surrounding the old country house.

"Topman thought that this house would be more private than a hospital. You're quite a hero here, Liam, for stopping the train. Every journalist in the United Kingdom wants to interview you."

O'Toole looked surprised. "But I didn't stop the train, Colonel. You did. You and Billy Two. If it hadn't been for you I'd be smeared across the walls of Victoria Station."

Barrabas shrugged. "Well, you know that and I know that, but..." He looked at O'Toole and smiled. "There's nothing like being a hero in your own hometown."

"Where are the rest of the boys now?"

"Bishop had to get back to Canada and Starfoot had some pressing business in the Arizona desert. Indian-rights stuff. As for Alex and Nate, I believe they're out on the town."

"Which means no Irish girl from here to Dublin is safe," O'Toole concluded with a chuckle.

At the gates, Barrabas turned and drove toward Belfast.

"Where we going, Colonel?"

"It's a surprise."

The two men rode silently for a while. Finally Barrabas spoke.

"You know it was Seamus Killerbey who betrayed Thomas Murphy back when you were a teenager?"

"You're kidding?" O'Toole was genuinely surprised. "Then why..."

"Originally, I guess you were just his cover. Since you'd left Ireland he spread a story that you did it. Then events overtook him. Apparently the original plan was someone else's—Terry McHugh's. But he was shot by British soldiers two weeks ago. Killerbey took over.''

"That explains something he said to me at the farmhouse.''

"What was that?''

"He kept laughing and saying that this business of Thomas Murphy's betrayal was nothing. He as much as admitted he knew I didn't do it. And he said something about there being a better betrayer around than me.''

Barrabas was about to reply, but stopped himself. They drove for a while in silence again.

"Well, anyway, Liam, Major Topman is discreetly leaking the file on the Murphy case so the true identity of the informer will get out. It'll clear your name, and with luck it'll stop the IRA from making Seamus Killerbey into another martyr.''

They had arrived on the outskirts of Belfast. Barrabas turned in a driveway that led up to the parking lot of a big modern hospital.

O'Toole looked at him, momentarily panicked. "Is Susy...?''

"No, Liam. Susy's not here.'' Barrabas parked the car.

"Then what...?''

"Surprise,'' he said again. "Come on.''

The two men entered the building and rode the elevator to the fifth floor. Barrabas walked briskly down the corridor, past the nurses in their starched white uniforms, past ambulatory patients in bathrobes.

O'Toole saw a sign that directed them to the intensive care ward.

At the end of the hall, Barrabas stopped before an open door and stood aside. He looked at O'Toole without saying anything. Still puzzled, O'Toole looked into the room.

His mother lay on the hospital bed, thin, and gray, and for the second time that day, O'Toole saw a human life nourished by clear fluid flowing through plastic tubes hooked into veins in the arms. His mother's hair was almost white.

Sensing the presence of someone in the room, she opened her eyes. For all that her body had faded, her green eyes shone with the strength of will that Liam O'Toole had always remembered. She saw her son standing in the doorway.

"Liam," she said. She moved her arm toward him. He noticed the Belfast newspaper on the bedside table. It headlined the story of how he'd saved Belfast from the runaway train. "I'm sorry, Liam. Will you ever forgive your mother for what she's done to her son?"

Liam O'Toole walked slowly into the room. "Mum," he said. He knelt by the bed and took her tiny hand in his.

Barrabas closed the door and waited in the corridor.

LATER, BARRABAS AND O'TOOLE drove back to the country house in complete silence. There had been no words between the two men since O'Toole's simple "Thank you" when he left his dying mother's room. When they pulled up to the house, O'Toole spoke again.

"I want to call Susy now."

Barrabas showed him the telephone in a downstairs room. O'Toole dialed through the international operator. He heard the telephone ring in his wife's New Jersey home. There was no answer. He hung up.

"She must be out. Shopping or something." He shrugged and looked at the Colonel. He sounded as if he were trying to convince himself.

"Sure," Barrabas said.

Hatton appeared at the doorway.

"Well, you can expect a call here from a journalist who's trying to scoop all the other papers for Liam's personal story," she told them with a grin. "Your friend Major Topman phoned. He said he owed a favor to this journalist, so he gave him the number here."

"As long as he doesn't have the address, we'll be safe," Barrabas said.

O'Toole thought "safe" was a strange choice of words. Almost immediately the phone rang. It was the journalist. Before he realized what he was doing, O'Toole was giving him the interview. "Damned skillful, these buggers," he told the Colonel and Hatton, holding his hand over the mouthpiece.

THAT EVENING O'TOOLE PHONED his wife's number over and over, letting the phone ring until the international operator finally broke the connection. He paced the house, restless, and ate almost no dinner. Finally Hatton ordered him to bed.

"You'll lose that hand yet, Liam, if you push yourself. You're over the worst of it, but you're going to backslide if you don't rest. Now get to bed!"

The Colonel gave him a cold look, the kind that usually accompanied an order. O'Toole agreed, on the condition that the telephone be left in his room.

For a long time he lay back on the pillow, contemplating the ceiling. He wondered where his wife was and what she was doing. He drifted off in restless sleep. He awoke sometime later with a full moon shining in his window, filling the room with cold white light. He was bathed in sweat and his hand throbbed with pain. Hatton was right. He wasn't over the hump yet.

The phone was ringing.

He reached over, grabbed it and put it to his ear.

"Liam."

His heart missed a beat when he heard her voice.

"Susy! Oh, my God, Susy. Where are you?"

"I'm in Ireland, Liam, I..."

"Christ, Susy, I've been phoning you all day in New Jersey. What's happened? Oh, God, I'm glad you're all right."

"Oh, so am I, Liam. That you're alive. I was sick with worry. The men who were watching the house disappeared, and as soon as they did I came back. I caught the first flight and came back to find you.''

"Where are you, Susy?''

He heard her giggle. "I'm sorry. It's just that now that you're all right, what I did seems funny. I came back to the hotel. The castle. It was the only place I could think of to start looking for you.''

"I'm coming for you right now, Susy. There's a car here. It'll take me about four hours to drive.''

"Oh, Liam. I want you to come." Susy sounded breathless and eager. "Liam?''

"What is it?''

"Are your friends there?''

"The Colonel? Yeah. And Dr. Hatton.''

"Don't tell them. Let's make it a surprise for them, okay. I want you to come alone, Liam. I want to be alone with you for a while first.''

"Sure, Susy.''

"Come quickly.''

"As fast as I can.''

"I love you.''

"I love you, too.''

She hung up.

O'Toole leaped from the bed and immediately became dizzy, almost keeling over. Gotta take it a little slower, he thought. He wiped the night sweat from his face and dressed.

As silently as possible, he walked through the house to the front doors and let himself out. The keys were in the car but he decided not to start it until he was out of hearing distance from the house. He put in the clutch and shifted into first. Then he stepped out and put his shoulder against the frame of the car. The driveway was on a long slight incline to the front gates. The car rolled.

He jumped back inside and coasted out the gates onto the street before he started the car up. It was just after one o'clock. County Mayo was a good four hours away. He drove fast.

JUST BEFORE DAWN Liam O'Toole drove through the gates of Ashford Castle and parked in the driveway under the high turret near the front doors. He strode up the steps and into the elegant, high-ceilinged foyer. A sleepy clerk appeared at the desk.

"I'm looking for Susy O'Rourke—or O'Toole. My wife . . . from America."

"Ah, yes, Mr. O'Toole. She's expecting you. She's in 309."

"Thank you."

O'Toole crossed to the broad staircase and ran up, two steps at a time. The clerk watched him disappear. He picked up the house phone and dialed room 309.

O'Toole rapped on the stout oak door. He heard the rustle of bed clothes and footsteps. The door opened.

He felt weak when he saw her. The moonlight that flooded into the room glistened on her skin and her golden hair. The cool night breeze, blowing in the open window, swirled her long nightgown around her, outlining the slender curves of her body.

"Susy," he said with a sigh, drinking in her beauty. He'd been forced to travel a long hard road. This was his destination. He crossed the threshhold into the room and closed the door behind him.

"I'm glad you came," Susy said to him. She moved back into the room, leaving him standing near the door. She was acting strangely. This wasn't the welcome O'Toole had envisioned.

"What's the matter, Susy?"

She stood by the window, closing the long casements. "Come here, Liam. I'll tell you."

O'Toole walked toward her slowly, puzzled by her response.

She turned to face him. There was a gun in her hand and it was aimed at Liam O'Toole.

A door that led to an adjacent suite opened, and Darby O'Goole walked into the room. He still wore his cassock.

"You! You were with Killerbey at the farm!" O'Toole's long nightmare had begun again.

"It was all an incredible coincidence at first," Susy said coldly. "Us meeting through that classified ad in the personal column. It wasn't aimed at anyone in particular. I just needed a guy to satisfy my needs. You did that for me all right, Liam. In fact, you did that exceptionally well.

"But the fact that you were also Liam O'Toole, deserter and traitor of the Irish Republican Army—that was the big prize. We didn't waste any time making plans."

"But why..."

"Why? Why?" Susy trembled with rage, her voice frozen with cold anger. "Because you're responsible for the death of Thomas Murphy. You betrayed him to the British. And for that you are going to die."

O'Toole's voice fell to a bare whisper. "But why you?"

"Because Thomas Murphy was my brother."

A macabre chuckle fell from O'Goole's lips. "So now O'Toole the betrayer has been betrayed."

"It all worked out so well," Susy said with a venomous sneer. "At least until your friends showed up. Oh, you've cost us pretty, Liam. But now it looks like things are working out again. It's almost enough to make me agree with Father O'Goole here when he says that God is on our side."

"God?" Liam O'Toole raised his head. "Or the Devil?"

"Don't play games. It's not going to get you out of this now." The black hole of the gun eyed the Irish-American. He waited for the gun to blink.

"All our love, our promises to each other—they were all for this?"

"I did it for Ireland. Something you wouldn't understand."

O'Toole breathed deeply. He knew he was going to die. He was determined to do it with dignity, even if his murderers were little more than... He couldn't say it. Not about Susy. Not his wife, the woman he loved more than anything else in the world. Where was she now? She was not the woman with the gun. When he spoke, his voice purred out from the depths of him.

"Sure, and we'll keep killing one another in Ireland until we stand in fields of carnage with the bones of our people hanging from the corners of our mouths and our chins awash in Irish blood. Aye, that'll be the liberation of the Emerald Isle."

When it was time for the poet, it was time to die.

He held his hands out in a gesture of surrender.

"I loved you, Susy."

Susy fired.

The door crashed inward in a shower of splinters. Lee Hatton's arm swung out, her gun steadied by her other hand. She fired once.

The silenced gun popped.

A big red eye opened up on Susy's forehead. Death was instantaneous. Barrabas flew past her. Darby O'Goole ran into the adjoining room, searching for cover, for something, anything, a place to hide.

There was no sanctuary for the Devil, no shelter from the storm of Barrabas's bullets.

O'Goole turned, panic-stricken, just in time to see the tall, white-haired mercenary burst into the room. The muzzle flashed orange and spat death. A bloody red line opened up across the priest's black cassock. O'Goole turned around and clawed at the wall. There was no handhold. He slid slowly to the floor, leaving his bloody tracks down the wall. His arms trembled briefly. Then they stopped. His still eyes, frozen permanently in disbelief, stared at the ceiling.

"They're going to miss you in purgatory, Father. You're booked on the express to hell," Barrabas snarled, looking at the body.

He went back into the first room. Lee Hatton was bending over the body of Liam O'Toole, stripping back his shirt.

"He's conscious, Colonel."

Barrabas knelt beside O'Toole. The man's eyes were strangely calm. Tears dampened his cheeks. Even tough old soldiers cry. Christ, poor Liam, he thought. The day he's reconciled with his mother and absolved of crimes he never committed he's betrayed by the woman he loves.

Hatton quickly ripped O'Toole's shirt into strips and staunched the flow of blood. "Like most people, Susy thought people's hearts are located under their left breasts, instead of in the center of the torso," she said. "He's got a bullet through his lung. It's bad, but he'll live."

"Colonel." O'Toole's voice was weak and hoarse. He fixed his eyes on Barrabas's face. "How'd you know?"

"I knew for sure when you told me Susy was back in New Jersey. They must have faked that call you made to New Jersey somehow. I checked out the house before coming to Ireland. It was empty. And there was no luggage, nothing to indicate anyone had returned. And I found something there. A photograph. The man in it seemed familiar, but I couldn't put a name to him. Not until your sister told me about Tom Murphy.

Then I remembered. He made headlines when he was shot down. Susy was in the picture, too. I had Major Topman check her out a few days ago.''

"I know,'' O'Toole said slowly. "She told me Murphy was her brother.''

Barrabas nodded. "Rourke was a phony name she took when she went to the United States to work as an IRA agent arranging arms shipments. I knew the vendetta against you wasn't over. Not after a setup like that. It was a sure thing they'd come after you again. We hid out at the country house Topman gave us. And meanwhile, he gave the phone number to the mouthiest journalist in Ireland. They got hold of it, just as we'd planned.''

"And you were listening in when she phoned.''

"Yeah. We were about three seconds too late. Sorry.''

O'Toole looked at him, a light smile playing across his lips. "Thanks, Colonel.''

"Anytime.''

Barrabas stood up. There was commotion at the door as hotel officials arrived. Curious guests crowded into the corridor and poked their heads through the door. A police siren sounded outside. Lee Hatton stayed with the wounded man. Barrabas moved out as the world moved in.

Poor Liam, he thought.

For mercenaries, life was worse than hell.

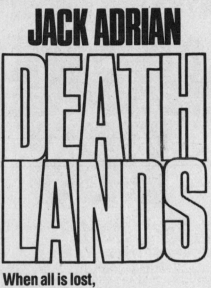

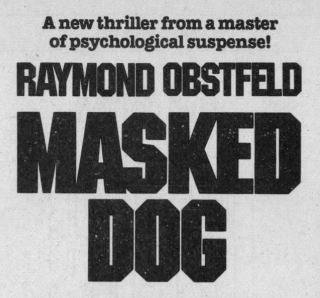

TAKE 'EM NOW

FOLDING SUNGLASSES FROM GOLD EAGLE

Mean up your act with these tough, street-smart shades. Practical, too, because they fold 3 times into a handy, zip-up polyurethane pouch that fits neatly into your pocket. Rugged metal frame. Scratch-resistant acrylic lenses. Best of all, they can be yours for only $6.99. **MAIL ORDER TODAY.**

Send your name, address, and zip code, along with a check or money order for just $6.99 + .75¢ for postage and handling (for a total of $7.74) payable to Gold Eagle Reader Service, a division of Worldwide Library. New York and Arizona residents please add applicable sales tax.

Remove from pouch...   unfold once...

unfold twice...   and they're ready to wear.

Gold Eagle Reader Service
901 Fuhrmann Blvd.
P.O. Box 1325
Buffalo, N.Y. 14240-1325

GES1-RR